TOO SLOW

Lancaster peered hard at Harland a moment and then he reached for his gun.

At the same instant that Lancaster's hand moved, Harland grabbed for his own weapon. He brought it out and up with all the speed and skill he possessed, but in that split second that the .44 was coming to a level, the awful, sickening realization hit Harland that he had been beaten. Lancaster's gun already was levelled. The big bore gaped at Harland's heart. All that Lancaster had to do was press the trigger. Harland knew he could never get his shot off in time.

.44

H. A. DeRosso

LEISURE BOOKS   NEW YORK CITY

A LEISURE BOOK®

February 1998

Published by special arrangement with Golden West Literary Agency.

Dorchester Publishing Co., Inc.
276 Fifth Avenue
New York, NY 10001

ISBN 0-8439-4357-2

Chapter One

The two riders working up the mountain towards the pass travelled about a mile apart. There was no hurry in their progress. The first rider made no effort to quicken his horse's pace and thus draw farther ahead. The second rider, too, seemed content with the rate he was travelling. He kept his distance, not trying at all to overtake the other, even though he had been hired to kill this first rider and intended to do so before nightfall.

This was lonely country through which they were proceeding. The pass cut a mammoth notch between the towering peaks that thrust their barren, ragged heights at the sky. The sun beat down but somehow, perversely, the higher the riders mounted the colder it got. The thinness of the air in some strange manner seemed to dilute most of the heat out of the sun's rays.

7

They had sighted no habitation that day and now that it was noon, the second rider, who was Dan Harland, decided that he might as well set about doing what he had been hired to do. So when Harland reached the mouth of the pass, he urged his bay on a little faster.

The pass was a narrow, twisting defile with sharply pitched walls. It was impossible to see very far ahead and thus Harland lost sight of the man he was following. Harland began to curse with vexation. The rider ahead, whose name was Jim Lancaster, should be aware that Harland was following him and for no good purpose. Therefore, Lancaster might halt at the first vantage point and wait in hiding until Harland was close enough to be dropped with a rifle shot.

The thought chilled Harland. He did not have much taste for what he was doing. It went against his conscience and peace of mind, but to Harland circumstances seemed to have dictated no other choice. So he moved up the pass, cautiously now, eyes slitted as he studied the pitch of the slopes and the floor of the pass ahead.

Dan Harland was twenty-seven years old and he stood an inch short of six feet. He had heavy shoulders but a slim waist and flat hips and slightly bowed legs that came from a lifetime in the saddle. He had his dreams and aims like all men and to Harland these ambitions had always seemed quite modest and reasonable. Perhaps that was where the fault lay, he often thought bitterly. Had he aspired greedily and ambitiously, he might not at this moment be engaged in doing something he so vehemently disliked.

There was a week's growth of tawny whiskers on Harland's face, and they could not quite conceal the bitter cast of his mouth nor the cold, harsh glint in his grey eyes. He wore a flannel-lined denim jacket and black woollen trousers tucked into the tops of his plain black boots. Belted about his waist was a wide shell belt, every loop filled with .44s. The belt supported a holster at Harland's right hip. The gun in the holster was a .44 Frontier Colt with a seven-and-a-half inch barrel.

Now the pass widened and straightened out for a bit and ahead of him Harland saw the man he was trailing. Harland reined in the bay abruptly, not quite able to understand what he saw.

Lancaster had stopped running. His horse stood with lowered head, grazing, and Lancaster was off to one side, facing the direction from which Harland was coming. Lancaster just stood there, clearly in the open. He made a perfect target.

Harland felt his throat constrict and for a moment the urge to turn and ride away from here assailed him. But the impulse quickly passed. He had taken this job and he intended carrying it out to its grim, brutal consummation. Still he hesitated, not so much out of reluctance or fear now, but rather out of caution.

Lancaster was far enough away to be out of six-shooter range. He seemed to stand there patiently, waiting for Harland to ride up. This did not make sense to Harland and the suspicion grew in him that this might be a trick. Yet when he scanned the land beyond Lancaster and on either side of him, there appeared to be nothing out of the ordinary. The ground was barren and so were the distant slopes. There was nothing behind which a man might lie in hiding.

Nevertheless, Harland's flesh crawled as he finally sent the bay ahead.

Lancaster did not move as Harland rode up. There

was a cigarette in Lancaster's mouth and he kept drawing on this and blowing the smoke slowly through his lips. He was using his left hand on the cigarette. Lancaster's right hand hung lax at his side, the fingers resting just below the tip of the tied-down holster that was snug against his thigh.

Harland reined in the bay about ten feet from Lancaster and for a while the two men stared at each other in silence. Lancaster was tall, standing two inches over six feet. He had a rather handsome face with piercing black eyes and black sideburns reaching halfway down his cheeks and a rich, black moustache curving down around the corners of his mouth. He seemed very thoughtful as he stared at Harland.

It was Lancaster who broke the silence. "Why don't you get off your horse, Harland?"

Harland stiffened a little in the saddle. "How do you know my name?" he asked.

Lancaster showed a small smile. "You're a famous gun-fighter, Harland. Everybody knows you. Didn't you beat Red Carleton to the draw and kill him in the San Martin Cattle War? Naturally, I've heard'about you, Harland. Why don't you dismount?"

It was all said blandly, but Harland thought he caught a faint note of mockery and derision in Lancaster's tone. Those dark eyes now seemed rather amused as they stared up at Harland.

As Harland sat there in the saddle, for the moment undecided, Lancaster raised the cigarette to his lips and drew on it again. He appeared to savour it immensely, the way he drew on it deeply and carefully, and the way he let the smoke come out of his mouth with an almost audible sigh of pleasure. It was almost as if Lancaster knew this was the last cigarette he would ever smoke.

It became apparent to Harland that Lancaster was not yet ready to have it out. Also, it was quite clear that there was no trickery involved for, had that been in Lancaster's mind, he could have selected a more appropriate place to make a treacherous stand. So, carefully, Harland swung his right leg back over the cantle of his kak and stepped to the ground.

Lancaster smiled. "I'm glad you dismounted," he said. "I wouldn't want to have an advantage over you. Or is it possible for anyone to have an advantage over the gunfighter who beat the great Red Carleton?"

A flare of anger beat against Harland's temples. He could never forget Red Carleton. It was this killing which had changed Dan Harland's whole life. It was this killing that had cast his existence into a hateful, distasteful pattern. He never liked to be reminded of it.

"What advantage are you talking about?" Harland growled.

"The advantage a man on the ground has in drawing his gun against a man on a horse," said Lancaster, arching a brow. "That's what you have in mind, isn't it, Harland? You're going to kill me, aren't you?"

Hearing it put baldly in words like that sent a paralysing chill down Harland's back. His throat went suddenly dry and the thought struck him that this was probably a trick after all. Lancaster knew what Harland had in mind, yet Lancaster had stopped running and had waited for Harland to come up. It just didn't tally up.

"All right," said Harland, "since you seem to know all about it, I am going to try to kill you." The words sounded harsh and brutal in his ears. "I'm giv-

11

ing you an even break. Any time you're ready, you can draw!"

"Even break?" echoed Lancaster in that mocking tone again. "How can anybody have an even break against the gunfighter who beat Red Carleton?"

The blaze of anger crossed Harland's mind again. He gritted his teeth against it and said, "You heard me. I'm waiting, Lancaster."

Suddenly the amusement and mockery went out of Lancaster. His face hardened. There was no fear in his eyes, only contempt. "All right, Harland. I'll oblige you. But I want to tell you something first. What makes you think you can beat me? Because you beat Red Carleton? Isn't it possible for someone else to be as good as Carleton or better? You think because you took Carleton you can take me. Is that why you're giving me what you call an 'even break'?"

"I'm not one to shoot a man in the back, Lancaster. I'm willing to take my chances face to face."

Lancaster cocked his head to one side and stared intently at Harland. "I believe you mean it," he said. "Well, I'm glad it's a man like you, Harland. I never did like the idea of a bullet in the back."

Harland said, "Are you going to draw?"

"Don't worry. I'll pull first," said Lancaster, that mocking smile touching his lips briefly. Then he sobered. His face grew pensive, as if he were immersed in profound thought, and what Lancaster was thinking about must not have been pleasant for Harland saw bitterness in the man's glance and in the set of his mouth. Lancaster took another deep drag on his cigarette and then he dropped the butt to the ground and carefully stamped it out with the toe of his boot. He lowered his head as he did this and he kept his head inclined, again giving the impression that he was going over something troubling in his mind. After a while, Lancaster raised his glance. His face appeared strained but resolute.

He peered hard at Harland a moment and then Lancaster reached for his gun.

At the same instant that Lancaster's hand moved, Harland grabbed for his own weapon. He brought it out and up with all the speed and skill he possessed, but in that split second that the .44 was coming to a level, the awful, sickening realisation hit Harland that he had been beaten. Lancaster's gun already was levelled. The big bore gaped at Harland's heart. All that Lancaster had to do was press the trigger. Harland knew he could never get his shot off in time.

Harland could see the dark yawn of eternity in the muzzle of Lancaster's .45. It was all so swift that there was not time for panic or fear or regret to formulate in Harland. He just felt sick and cold and then his .44 was at level and aimed and he had just begun to wonder why Lancaster did not fire when the .44 went off in his hand.

The bullet took Lancaster in the chest. The shock of it shivered him and a groan began to rip out of him but he clenched his teeth over the agony and stifled the outcry. As if in silent, accusing mockery, the .45 in his fist pointed a moment longer, unfired, at Harland's heart. Then the hand holding the weapon wavered. Lancaster's head fell down over his breast. His legs weakened and he went down on one knee. He was a while like that, staring mutely at the gun he had not used and which he still gripped. He opened his fingers, allowing the weapon to fall, and then Lancaster folded over gently on his side and hit the ground.

Harland's heart beat like a throbbing drum in his

ears. Within him, he could hear a tiny, forlorn voice crying dismally against the whole thing. But he knew it was done and beyond recall. He felt sick and miserable. He wanted desperately to crawl out of it somehow.

There seemed to be water in his belly as he dropped to his knees and turned Lancaster over on his back. Lancaster lay very still and on the instant Harland thought the man was dead. But the blood kept flowing out of the wound in Lancaster's breast and then his lips fluttered ever so slightly as he breathed.

"Lancaster," Harland tried to say, but the word only strangled in his throat and emerged as an unintelligible sound. "Lancaster." This time Harland got it out but the man did not answer. His eyes remained closed and his breast barely stirred as he breathed. He looked strangely peaceful, as if in the bliss of untroubled sleep, but the blood staining his shirt gave the lie to this.

"Lancaster," Harland said once more.

There was no reply. The awesome silence of the mountains closed in about Harland, seeming to squeeze and stifle his heart. The only sound he heard was the loud noise of his own breathing.

Harland did what he could for Lancaster. He bared Lancaster's breast and bandaged the wound. Harland did not expect this to do any good but he could not bring himself to stand around idly and watch the man die. The irony of this struck a grim amusement in him for a moment, for he had done his best to kill Lancaster and now that the man was dying, Harland did not want it so. Yet it was the circumstances of the man's death, not the death itself, that troubled Harland.

By all rights he, Dan Harland, should be the man on the ground with a bullet wound in his breast that was spilling the life out of him. He had been beaten to the draw. If Lancaster had fired, he could have dropped Harland with ease. But for some strange, unbelievable reason, Lancaster had withheld his fire. He had deliberately allowed Harland to kill him.

While Harland worked on him, Lancaster's eyes remained closed. There was only the smallest hope in Harland that Lancaster would ever regain consciousness, and there was no hope at all that Lancaster would live.

When he was through with the wound, Harland covered Lancaster with a blanket from his bedroll. Then Harland unsaddled Lancaster's horse and propped the wounded man's head on his kak. Through all this Lancaster's eyes stayed shut. Only his breathing, which now began to come loud and harsh and irregular, indicated that he was still alive.

Harland tried telling himself that it was no good to get upset. The thing was done. There was no going back in time and avoiding it. He had shot Lancaster and the man was going to die and that was that. He would just have to accept it whether he liked it or not.

But his mind refused to become accustomed to something as brutal and as callous as this. He had killed before and he supposed that in time he would kill again, but he had never before taken another man's life without provocation or in self-defence. He had deliberately hired out to kill Lancaster. Now all that remained was for him to go back and draw his pay. The thought made Harland sick to his stomach.

After a while, Harland went over to Lancaster and peered down at the dying man. Lancaster seemed not to have stirred. At times his breathing was loud and strained. Then it would fade and appear to stop and just when Harland was sure the man was dead, Lancaster would begin to breathe heavily again.

Harland could not endure the waiting. He told himself he did not have to hang around. He could pick up and go at any moment. Lancaster would die whether Harland stayed or left. But Harland could not bring himself to leave. He had to remain here as long as there was any chance that Lancaster might return to consciousness for there was something Harland wanted to learn from the man. There could be no peace in Harland's mind unless he learned that thing.

The next time he looked at the dying man he saw that Lancaster's eyes were open and watching him.

Harland came ahead a couple of steps so that he stood beside Lancaster. The eyes looked straight up at Harland.

A pulse was pounding in Harland's throat. "Can you hear me, Lancaster?" he asked.

Lancaster's mouth moved as a weak smile came over it. He gazed up at Harland as if he were aware of the consternation and torment in Harland's mind and was amused by it. Lancaster said nothing. He gave a small, barely perceptible nod.

"Can you talk, Lancaster?" asked Harland.

"Of course I can talk." It was said plainly though weakly. The amusement grew in Lancaster's eyes. The smile broadened for a moment, then it was swiftly erased by a spasm of pain that left the man's face very grey and his eyes luminous with hurt.

Harland dropped to one knee beside Lancaster. "Why did you hold your fire?" Harland asked. "Why did you let me shoot first?"

Lancaster's eyes closed and a breath rattled in his

16

throat. For the moment Harland feared that the man had dropped off again, but then Lancaster's eyes opened and stared blandly up at Harland.

"I don't know what you mean, Harland."

"You beat me to the draw," said Harland, feeling sweat running down his cheeks. He had thought all the turmoil was within him. He was surprised that it should show outwardly on him. He balled his fingers so as not to betray any possible trembling. "You could have dropped me easy. But you didn't shoot. Why?"

Lancaster's eyes squinted a little as he gazed up. That small smile came over his mouth again. He paused a moment and then he said, "Don't be silly, Harland."

"You let me kill you," Harland said. "You had that in your mind when you stopped and waited for me to catch up with you. You had me cold but you held your fire. I want to know why, Lancaster."

"You're talking crazy, Harland."

"Stop trying to pretend it wasn't so," Harland said stiffly. "I know what I saw. You had your gun out before mine but you waited for me to shoot first."

"Did I?" said Lancaster, and turned his face away.

The feeling began to grow in Harland that he would never get Lancaster to admit the fact. So Harland tried something else. "Who wants you dead, Lancaster?"

Lancaster kept his face averted. His voice sounded very tired. "Don't you know? Weren't you hired to kill me?"

A twinge passed through Harland's heart. "The party who hired me made it clear that he was just acting for someone else. Who is that someone, Lancaster?"

"You're a funny one, Harland," Lancaster said

slowly. "You hire out to kill me and as soon as you've done it you begin to feel sorry. Now you want to know who ordered me killed. Do you have a crazy idea of trying to square things by killing whoever it was that had me killed?

"I've got some advice for you, Harland. Get into some other work. You're not cut out for a hired killer. You've got a conscience. You'll kill but you've got to have a reason for it. You're in the wrong business, Harland."

With that, Lancaster turned his face away. His breathing quickened, it came loud and insistent now. Harland bent over a little and saw that Lancaster's eyes were closed. He called Lancaster's name softly. The man did not answer. Harland called again, louder. There was no reply. Lancaster was in a coma again.

Night fell and Lancaster still lived. Harland built a fire as close as he dared to the dying man so that he might catch a little heat since with sundown a vicious chill had descended on the mountain. The stars came out and glittered with an indifferent, malevolent brightness. Somewhere up the pass a coyote began to cry.

Harland ate nothing that night. He made himself some coffee and drank that. It was all that his stomach would take.

Every now and then he would go over beside Lancaster and look down at the dying man. Lancaster had not regained consciousness since he had dropped off this second time. He just lay there in his troubled sleep, the breath at times harsh and sibilant as it gusted out of him. At other times his breathing was so silent and invisible as to make Harland think the man was dead. But when Harland felt for the pulse, he found it beating every time.

Several times Lancaster mumbled in his delirium. Harland tried to listen closely to this in the hope of learning that which he wanted to know. But Lancaster's mind was back in his childhood. He talked about his mother a lot. Once he shouted for her quite clearly.

Harland had just started to doze off when Lancaster's shout wakened him. Harland looked towards Lancaster and saw that the man was sitting upright, glaring straight ahead of him with wild, distended eyes. Lancaster shouted his mother's name a second time and then he fell back.

Lancaster had died with his head turned to one side. The eyes were shut and the mouth was closed. Even in death the curve of his lips held a small, weary bitterness.

Chapter Two

Back in San Martin County, Dan Harland had been a cowboy. He had worked for the Pothook outfit and he had been quite contented. In common with other young men engaged in the same vocation in that year of 1878, Harland had had the simple dream of some day owning his own ranch. Nothing pretentious, Harland had dreamed, just a section or two and a few head of cattle. He had never expected to compete with the cattle barons.

Afterwards, as he matured in years and acquired a rather cynical wisdom, Harland thought it strange that because he had always aspired to only a little he had been denied even the tiniest part of it, whereas those who possessed a lot were never satisfied with what they had but were forever seeking to get more.

It was this greed and cupidity in the men who had a lot that brought about the San Martin Cattle War.

Harland was never sure just how that bloody feud started. He became involved because he worked for Pothook, which was one of the two large ranches in San Martin County. The other large outfit was Running W. Harland knew many of the Running W boys and he had helled around with them in town. He had had nothing against them.

First there was talk of grazing rights and water rights. Talk became argument and argument in time erupted into violence. Harland had been quite bewildered by all of it. He could not understand why the Running W boys who once had been pretty decent chaps should now be held up as devils incarnate and his bitter enemies. But he worked for Pothook and, confused as he was, he just went helplessly along with it.

It was not the cowpunchers, however, who precipitated most of the violence but the hired gunmen who were brought in by both Pothook and Running W. One of the gunmen who hired out to Running W was named Red Carleton.

Carleton was a blowmouth who claimed that he had killed fourteen men. Whether this was an exact tally no one had ever taken the trouble to find out. However, that Carleton had killed several men there was no doubt. He was forever looking for trouble as an excuse to kill again so that he might add to his gory prestige. It was almost like a game to Carleton. It made him feel like a champion to be able to claim that he had killed more men in gun duels than anyone else.

So it came to pass that one day Red Carleton took on Dan Harland. The two had never met before this day but since one man worked for Running W and the other for Pothook, this fact supposedly made them mortal enemies. It was a chance encounter in town and Harland would have just passed it up, but Carleton had other ideas.

Perhaps it was because Carleton was innately cruel and compassionless. Or perhaps it was because in an inexperienced cowboy like Harland, Carleton saw an easy addition to his imposing list of victims. So the two men shot it out.

It was true that Dan Harland was packing a gun that day, but he always packed a six-shooter. He had carried one even before the San Martin Cattle War had broken out. It was the custom of the time and Harland would just as soon have walked down the main drag of any town naked as to have gone out without his .44. So just because Harland was packing a gun did not mean he was asking for trouble.

Until that moment, Harland had never pulled his gun against a fellow man. He had in the past used his .44 quite a bit. He had killed jack-rabbits with it and a couple of coyotes that had come in range of the weapon. He was also very adept at picking tin cans off the tops of fence posts and he had also used the butt of the weapon on occasion to shoe a horse. But he had never intended using the gun to kill a fellow-being.

As it turned out, Harland beat Red Carleton to the draw and killed him. Just exactly how it happened, Harland never knew. He never bothered very much to figure it out, either. He knew now that he was good with a gun and as a result he was fair game for any glory hunter who could add to his stature by boasting that he had killed Dan Harland who had killed Red Carleton who had killed Kid Bisbee who had killed—

In the next year Harland was forced to kill two

other gunmen whose only reason for trying to kill him was to augment their cruel and bloody prestige. After this initiation into the ways of gunmen, Harland found that he had earned the name, whether he liked it or not.

He spent the next three years of his life trying to get away from it, but it was no go. He was Dan Harland. He was fast with a gun. He was a killer.

It was surprising how his reputation got around. He tried changing his name but it always seemed that eventually someone who had known him in San Martin County or elsewhere spotted him and then the truth would come out. He tried drifting but that didn't help either. He was a marked man.

Harland found that with his new reputation only one kind of work was available to him. Whenever he was hired he was expected to use his gun. It was not always put as baldly as that. He would be employed ostensibly to punch cows but invariably a situation would arise which would call for him to use his .44. So Harland would quit because hiring out his gun was against his principles. This left him out of a job and he would seek employment elsewhere.

Harland stood as much of it as he could. The day eventually came that Dan Harland got filled right up to the top of his throat. He was sick of the hypocrisy and deceit. He was sick of being shoved around. If he was a gunman, he would live like a gunman. He shoved his principles and ideas as far back as he could in his mind. It was then that he took on the job of tracking down and killing one James Lancaster. . . .

After he had buried Lancaster, Harland rode to the small settlement of Los Pinos where he was to meet the man who had hired him, one Buckskin Tom Elliott. Los Pinos lay in a small bowl ringed by lofty mountain crests. Ponderosa pines grew straight and huge on the mountain slopes. The grama grass brushed its tops against Harland's stirrups. It was good cow country.

Harland got to Los Pinos in the afternoon and he immediately started a canvass of the six saloons of the settlement, for a saloon was Buckskin Tom Elliott's natural habitat. It was in the fifth saloon that he looked into that he found Elliott. The man was in his glory. He had a foot propped on the brass rail and an elbow hooked on the bar and in his other hand he held a bottle of whisky and he was holding forth on the days of his youth when he had hunted the buffalo on the plains.

A faint revulsion stirred in Harland as he walked up to the bar. He had just lifted his boot on the rail when Elliott noticed him. Elliott's voice halted in the middle of a sentence. His eyes, once they had rested on Harland, never moved from him.

The bartender came up and Harland ordered whisky. The barman poured and when Harland tossed a coin on the bar, Elliott's voice came. "Take it out of here, Ted."

The bartender looked inquiringly at Harland.

"Why not?" said Harland, and downed his drink.

Elliott did not resume his tale although he had left it dangling in mid-air. He kept on staring at Harland. Harland finally turned his head and glanced directly at Elliott.

"Hello, Elliott," he said.

Elliott raised the bottle in his left hand and took a deep swallow. He looked like he was bursting to say something but he kept himself in check. With exaggerated casualness he sighed loudly and wiped his mouth with the back of his hand. He belched heartily and started towards Harland. One of the barflies hurriedly downed his shot and plucked at Elliott's sleeve as he passed by. Elliott turned on the man with a snarl, then caught himself and motioned the bartender to serve another round. Then Elliott walked up to Harland.

Elliott nodded his head at a table in the far corner of the barroom. "Join me, Harland?" he said.

They sat down at the table. Elliott leaned both elbows on the table and peered intently at Harland. The bottle in Elliott's left hand was half empty but the man did not look drunk. He had a glow on but he still retained complete possession of his faculties.

"Well, Harland?" he said at last when Harland made no move to speak.

Harland reached in a shirt pocket and took out a ring and tossed it on the table. Elliott snatched it up in a dirty hand with a vile eagerness. He began turning the ring around in his fingers and chortling.

"Just what I wanted. This is just what I wanted." His back was to the bar and he winked broadly at Harland. "Come out to my place and I'll pay you for this. What a lovely ring! Shall we go right away, Harland?"

Harland nodded. He was sad and sick inside.

They reached Elliott's place after darkness had set in. When he called the place his, Elliott used the possessive loosely. In reality the place was an abandoned line-shack that Elliott had appropriated for his own use while he stayed in this part of the country.

"How did it go, Harland?" he asked.

"Not bad."

"You have any trouble?"

"No."

The man's eyes burned as if from a wicked fever. "How did you get him?" he asked. He was almost drooling with anticipation.

"I called him and beat him to the draw," said Harland.

"Just like that?"

"Yes."

"Haw-haw-haw," roared Elliott. He threw back his head and slapped his thigh. "Haw-haw-haw." He banged the table with the flat of his hand and then he began to wipe his eyes. "Haw-haw-haw," he said, a little more subdued now.

"What's so damn funny?" Harland asked thinly.

"Oh, Harland," Elliott chuckled, still wiping at his eyes, "who are you trying to josh! I'm not the law. I'm on the same side you are." He gave that broad wink, working one side of his mouth at the same time, in a display that was almost obscene the way he performed it. "I'm your friend. I won't tell. Come on," he said, leaning forward confidentially and eagerly. "Tell me. Just how did you get Lancaster?"

Harland felt his stomach turn. For a moment he froze there, incredulous, not quite able to understand how a thing as sordid and brutal as this could get such a grip on a man. This was Elliott's whole life, this was meat and drink to him, this business of killing and revelling in its details. Harland felt very ill for having become associated with a man as evil as Elliott.

"I guess you killed him all right," Elliott said. "You never would have got this ring from Jim Lancaster if he wasn't dead. But you can't blame me for laughing, Harland. You beat Jim Lancaster to the draw?" He was frankly dubious.

"He's dead, isn't he?"

Elliott made an irritated gesture. "All right, have it your way. Go on pretending that you beat Lancaster, but that doesn't mean I have to believe you. Lancaster was real good with a gun." He tossed the packet of money on the table but Harland made no move towards it. "Here's the rest of it," Elliott went on. "You can count it if you're afraid it's not all there."

He settled back in his chair and folded his hands over his waist. "I'm going to do you a favour, Harland," he said charitably. "You might have been foolish enough to stand up to Lancaster and lucky enough to get away with it, so I am going to do you a favour." His eyes narrowed and glittered cruelly. "Does it really make any difference how a man gets it, Harland? He winds up dead, doesn't he? He's just as dead whether you give it to him from the front or from the back." He gave that coarse, exaggerated wink again. "In this business, you can't be too careful about your own skin, Harland. Why take chances?"

"Is that how you go about it, Elliott?"

"Why not?" Elliott shrugged. "I've got to be fifty-three years old that way. That's a lot older than you'll ever get, Harland, if you keep standing up to a man face to face."

"Thanks for the advice," Harland said dryly. He could not stand any more of Elliott's company. He had to get out of this shack and out of Elliott's proximity. But first Harland had one more thing to do.

He rose to his feet and went over to the table and picked up the money. He did not glance at it. Hurriedly, he shoved it in a pocket.

"You never told me, Elliott," he said as casually as he could, "just who it is that wanted Lancaster dead?"

"That's right," said Elliott, "I never told you."

Their eyes locked. Defiance and mockery glittered in Elliott's yellow-tinged glance. "I'd like to know," Harland said quietly.

"Why?"

"I'd just like to know who I was really working for."

Elliott leaned forward with an elbow on the table. His manner was cold and menacing. "Look, Harland," he said softly, "if whoever it was that hired me to hire someone to kill Lancaster had wanted you to know him, he would have hired you himself, wouldn't he? You've been paid, Harland. Go have yourself a good time and when you're broke look me up and I'll fix you up again with something that will earn you a few easy dollars."

"All right, Elliott," he said, his lips pale, "you don't have to tell me. There are other ways to find out. Lancaster was from Edenville, wasn't he? Well, I'm going to mosey over to Edenville and just nose around a while. Who knows? Maybe I'll find just what I'm looking for."

"Stay away from Edenville," said Elliott. His right hand lay out of sight beneath the table. His left elbow was still hooked on the edge.

"Who's to keep me from going there?" asked Harland, jeering. "You, Elliott?"

For a moment Elliott sat there tense and menacing, his eyes glaring at Harland. Then Elliott relaxed. He smiled. "All right, Harland," he said pleasantly. "It's a free country. Go to Edenville. I wish you luck." He was openly deriding.

Harland's throat was tight but he got the words out even and unruffled. "Hasta la vista, Elliott," he murmured and turned his back and headed for the door.

He took two steps and then he whirled with his .44 whipping up in his hand. He had not misjudged Elliott. The man still sat at the table but he had finally brought his right hand up above the surface. The hand held Elliott's big Remington.

Elliott evidently had had supreme confidence in his skill at deceit. Shock and consternation slacked his features as Harland whirled, gun in hand, and then panic came, wild and terrifying, as Elliott realised his treachery had not been swift enough.

Harland's first shot crashed into Elliott's chest. He cried out harshly and folded up over the table. But he still clung to his .44-40 and after an instant he began to come up, gun extended, pain-filled eyes seeking Harland.

Harland fired again. This bullet caught Elliott and hurled him back. He hit the floor on the nape of his neck, screaming, his legs thrashing, but he still had fight left in him. He hunched himself up into a ball and rolled on his side. He shoved his right arm out and, resting it on the ground to steady his aim, pointed the Remington at Harland.

Harland fired a third time. This slug ripped a tortured groan out of Elliott. The Remington fell unfired from his hand. He rolled on his back. His breath would not come and he began to claw at his shirt and then at his neck. All this brought him was a bubble of blood out of his gasping mouth.

Harland came ahead until he stood over Elliott. He looked down into Elliott's straining eyes and horrible red mouth and said, ''Thanks for telling me how you worked, Elliott. It saved my life.''

Then Harland stood there and watched. For the first time in his life he experienced no regret as he watched a man die.

Chapter Three

This range of mountains in which Edenville lay was known as the Stalwarts. Like practically all of the mountain ranges of the West it ran north and south, with, of course, an occasional spur or ridge striking off diagonally from the main range, but the backbone of the mountain extended north and south.

Edenville lay in the centre of a broad valley. The graze was good here and as a consequence all the land was taken up by ranches. Harland counted five different brands as he came down this mountain slope and cut across the valley towards Edenville.

Harland rode his bay at a walk in between the buildings, looking for a place to stay, for he had a feeling that he would be in and about Edenville a while. When he came to the Lamar House, Harland figured it was as good a place as he'd find in town and so he registered there.

Up in his room, Harland stripped and washed himself down with the water in the porcelain basin on the chest of drawers. After he had dressed in clean clothing out of his pack, he lay on his bed. The beard on his face itched and he intended getting a haircut and shave, but he wanted to lie on his bed a while first and think.

It did not take him long to go over what he had in mind for there was very little to begin with. Just the knowledge that Jim Lancaster had lived here in Edenville, but that did not necessarily mean anything. The person who had ordered Lancaster's death did not have to be from Edenville. The only other scrap of information that Harland had he had found in Buckskin Tom Elliott's pockets after the man had died. This was a letter addressed to Elliott at Los Pinos, General Delivery, from a woman named Lily who in the course of the letter had mentioned that she still worked in Ace's place. The letter had been postmarked Edenville.

It was the middle of the afternoon when Harland walked out of the Lamar House. He entered the first barbershop he came to and had the beard taken from his face and his hair trimmed. He paused a while, studying his clean face in the barber's mirror and wondering if it was the face of a killer. The cheeks were gaunt and his mouth seemed to have thinned. The eyes were cold and cynical. He had the look of a killer all right, and Harland's heart was sick as he went out into the sunlight.

He strolled through Edenville until he found what he was looking for. The saloon had a sign which read THE ACE OF DIAMONDS, ACE LOWRIE PROP. Harland did not enter. Edenville still drowsed, except for some minor activity at the two general stores and the stables and the blacksmith shop. What Harland was looking for would come out only in the evening and the hours of darkness. So he went back to the Lamar House to wait.

He came out into the air again just as night had taken over the valley. The sky was still clear and Harland could see the stars glittering overhead. It reminded him of how they had glittered, cold and distant and indifferent, that night while he had waited for Jim Lancaster to die. With a nettled curse, Harland put the thought from his mind. He should not keep thinking about Lancaster, he told himself. If he had refused the job, Elliott would have hired someone else to kill Lancaster. In any event, Lancaster would have died.

Harland stopped in a small eating-place for supper. Then he struck out for the Ace of Diamonds, taking his time as he walked along, savouring to the full his after-supper smoke.

The Ace of Diamonds no longer slumbered. Lights blazed inside and through the swing doors came the sounds of talk and laughter and music. Harland pushed the swing doors aside and entered this world of hilarity and amusement and, in some cases, sombre regret.

The Ace of Diamonds had a goodly crowd. Harland supposed that on Saturday nights it did much better than this but for a weekday night Ace Lowrie, whoever he was, should have no complaints. The long bar was half-filled and there was a poker game going and the percentage girls seemed to be doing all right.

The bar ran the length of one wall. The remainder of the ample barroom was filled with tables and chairs. In the back of the barroom was a stairway that led upstairs. At the foot of the stairway was a tiny platform just a foot higher than the floor. A piano was on the platform and someone was playing this while a woman with a throaty voice sang. She sang about a cowboy who had a sweetheart and while he was away with a trail-herd he left his sweetheart in the care of his best pal only to return home and find that his best pal had married his sweetheart. It was supposed to be very sad.

Before Harland had quite reached the bar he was met by one of the girls. She flashed a painted smile at him and said, "Buy me a drink, cowboy?"

Lowrie's girls certainly didn't lose time, Harland thought wryly. He put an elbow on the bar and looked at the woman closely She smiled again at his interest in her. She had on a tight dress with a short skirt and she kept one hand on her hip while with the other she toyed with the artificial curls in her bronze hair.

"Your name Lily?" asked Harland.

She frowned in instant resentment. Then she put on that crimson smile again and moved in close until she pressed against him. "My name's Rose," she said. "You don't need Lily when Rose is around, honey. Aren't you going to buy me a drink?"

Harland signalled one of the two bartenders. The bartender poured whisky out of one bottle for Harland and for the girl, Rose, he used another bottle, the colour of whose liquid was that of whisky but Harland presumed it was just tinted water. But he did not mind. He saluted Rose with his shot glass and downed the whisky. He signalled the bartender for another round for himself and the girl.

Rose snuggled close to him. "I like your style, handsome," she cooed. "You sure know how to treat a girl good."

Harland put an arm around her shoulders. "This is

33

just the beginning of it, honey," he said. "I'm out to tree the town tonight. How about sending Lily to me?"

"Say," said the girl, getting angry and pulling away from him, "what are you so hot after Lily for, huh? Come to think about it, I ain't ever seen you around before. How do you know there's a Lily works here?"

Harland told the bartender to set up another drink for Rose. This mollified her somewhat and when Harland smiled at her she pouted in mock hurt. "It's like this, honey," he said. "A pal of mine passed through Edenville once and he got kind of stuck on Lily. He asked me if I ever came through here to say hello to her for him." He winked at Rose. "I just want to keep my promise. From what my pal told me about Lily I don't think she's so hot. You've got it all over her, honey. Now be a good girl and send Lily to me so I can say hello to her and have the rest of the night to spend with you. How about it?"

That carmine smile flashed brighter than ever. "Just like you say, handsome. Don't be too long," she cooed, and went off with hips swinging.

Lily approached with the come-on discarded from her manner. She did not expect to realise any gain from this encounter and so she displayed no pretence at geniality and welcome. She came up to Harland and stared at him hard for a moment.

"Rose said you wanted to see me."

"Is your name Lily?"

"That's what I'm called. Lily Sinclair. What do you want, cowboy? I don't know you."

Lily was a blonde. Harland would have put her age in the early thirties. She was rather heavy with large breasts and prominent hips and for those men who liked substance to their women Harland supposed she was ideal. It was hard to tell what her face was really like under the thick layer of powder and rouge. The mouth was small and round and pursed tightly now as she watched him with a calculating glint in her pale blue eyes.

"Could I talk to you alone?" asked Harland.

"Is this business, cowboy?"

"Not what you mean by business. I want you alone to talk to you."

"Talk about what?"

"A pal of mine you wrote a letter to once. The letter was addressed to Los Pinos."

He could not have had a more marked effect on her if he had slapped her in the face. In an instant the defiance swept from her. Her eyes looked shocked and then frightened. Her shoulders slumped. After a moment, however, she regained a measure of composure.

"We can sit at a table," she said, and led the way.

When they were seated, she said tightly, "I can't be long, mister. I've got to stay on the job. Say what you have to say in a hurry."

Harland leaned back in his chair and stared narrowly across the table at Lily. For the benefit of whoever might be looking, she tried to give the appearance of being hard at work. She leaned forward intimately so that her breasts hung over the table, and put on a smile for him. But the smile did not quite come off. It was too singular in its fixity. It looked more like a grimace.

"What was Buckskin Tom Elliott to you?" he asked quietly.

"It's none of your business."

"You asked him for money in that letter you

35

wrote," said Harland. "You asked when he was coming back to you. Were you married to him?"

"What's the big idea?" she said. The smile was gone now. Her face twitched. "First you kill Tom and then you come here asking questions about him. Just what are you up to, Harland?"

His eyes narrowed to slits. He could hear the hard thumping of his heart. "How come you know my name?"

"You must be Dan Harland. I heard he was in town so you must be him."

"Who told you I killed Elliott?"

She raised a hand and began fingering her bare throat. "It's common talk around town. They say you were seen riding out of Los Pinos with Tom. Then Tom was found dead and they say you were the one who killed him."

"Did anyone see me kill him?"

"I don't know."

"Who were Elliott's friends?" asked Harland.

"I don't know what you mean."

"Who were his pals? Who did he talk to, who did he loaf around with, who did he do business with?" said Harland, his voice low and vicious. The anger was pounding behind his eyes.

"He—Tom knew lots of people," she moaned. "Oh, please, don't make me talk about him."

"What do you know about Jim Lancaster?" Harland asked, a trifle more gently.

She raised her head at that and looked him square in the eyes. The terror mounted in her glance and for an instant he thought she was going to cry out. Then she shoved her fist against her mouth and clamped her teeth on a finger. She sat like that, eyes full of an immeasurable fear and loathing looking at him as if he were something unclean.

"Lancaster lived in Edenville," Harland went on when Lily did not speak. "He must have come into this place now and then. Didn't you know him?"

She just stared at him.

"Why are you scared like this?" asked Harland, strongly curious. "What was there between Elliott and Lancaster? Why don't you say something?"

The terrible fascination of her stare finally broke. She looked past Harland and all at once that mechanical smile parted her mouth and she was saying:

"If you want me to keep on talking with you, cowboy, you'll have to buy me another drink."

Harland turned and saw the two men who had come up behind him. He scraped his chair back a little and to the side so as to face them. One of the men said, "Someone at the bar wants you, Lily."

"Sure, Ace, sure," she said, getting hurriedly to her feet. She seemed relieved to be able to get away from there.

Ace Lowrie stood an even six feet tall. He was rather slim and pale, but, looking at him, Harland had the impression that all this was deceiving. The man was hard and competent, despite his appearance. His black hair was slicked down and a thin black moustache graced his upper lip. He wore a black broadcloth coat and a flowered vest and grey trousers and expensive, highly-polished, black boots. A shell belt slanted across his waist but the gun and holster were hidden behind a fold of the long-tailed coat. He did not look like a man who lived a strenuous life but there was steel in him, Harland decided.

Lowrie had non-committal brown eyes that had a

way of regarding a man with absolute disinterest. He laid this stare on Harland and after a while Lowrie said, "Looks like you're out to give my girls a bad time tonight, Harland."

"Are you Lowrie?" asked Harland.

"That's right."

"How did you know my name?"

Lowrie permitted himself a faint smile. "Word gets around when we have a famous visitor in Edenville. You registered at the Lamar House, didn't you? You used your right name, didn't you?" He gave a small shrug. "That's how I know who you are, Harland."

Harland said nothing. He could feel the irritation and the anger begin deep in him. It was always like this when the matter of his notoriety was brought up. To avoid flying off the handle, he said nothing.

Lowrie shoved his hands into his pockets and teetered a little on his toes. "What did you want with Lily, Harland?"

"I wanted to buy her a drink and maybe take her upstairs," said Harland blandly. "That's what you're in business for, isn't it, Lowrie?"

A small pinpoint of anger glared in each of Lowrie's eyes. His lips tightened ever so slightly. "Are you trying to be funny, Harland?"

"You're the one asking the questions, Lowrie. I'm only giving you the answers."

"He's tough, Ace," said Lowrie's companion. "Don't you know? He's the great Dan Harland."

It was said dryly and mockingly. Harland shifted his glance and laid it on the man who stood just half a step behind and to the right of Lowrie. This fellow was blond and slight. He was dressed like a dandy. There was a cream-coloured Stetson on his head. A yellow silk scarf was wrapped around his neck. His shirt was a bright red and over this he wore a black and white calfskin vest. The legs of his pearl-grey trousers were tucked into the tops of fancy Cheyenne boots. His spurs were huge, ornate Mexican affairs that jingled loudly with every step he took. The cartridge belt about his middle had a lot of white stitching and so did the holster which also had a large silver concha embedded in its centre. The gun in the holster was a pearl-handled, silver-plated Colt .45. The tip of the holster was tied down with a thong to the fellow's thigh. Harland paid especial attention to how this hardware was worn.

Without taking his glance off Harland, Lowrie said, "Stay out of this, Dude."

Lowrie pulled out a chair and sat down facing Harland. "Why have you come to Edenville, Harland?" asked Lowrie.

"What makes you think I'm going to answer that?"

"I told you he was tough," said Dude with a sneer.

"Cut it out, Dude," said Lowrie with a faint show of anger. Dude flushed but he made no move to go away. His eyes went on contemplating Harland.

Lowrie leaned an elbow on the table. There was no resentment or irritation in his voice. "You're right, Harland," he agreed. "You don't have to answer. But, frankly, I'm curious. You kill both Elliott and Lancaster and then you come here to Edenville. It doesn't make sense."

"Who says I killed Elliott and Lancaster?" growled Harland.

Lowrie showed a faint smile. "When you run a saloon, Harland, you hear lots of gossip. I'm only repeating what I heard. The way the talk goes they are quite sure it was you who did in Buckskin Tom

Elliott although there was no one around to see it and so they can't prove it. There is also talk that Jim Lancaster is dead and that you were hired to kill him. Is that true?''

"Come now, Lowrie, you don't expect me to answer that!''

Lowrie showed his teeth in a sudden grin. "I keep forgetting myself. I guess I sound a lot like a prosecuting attorney.'' The smile vanished and he became quite serious. "Frankly, Harland, I'm interested in Lancaster because I knew him. Now I'm not trying to pump you, I'm not taking sides. But I would like to know if he's dead.''

"If I had killed him, would I have come to Edenville?'' asked Harland.

Lowrie paused and stared thoughtfully at Harland. After a while, Lowrie said, "You won't tell me if you know whether Jim Lancaster is dead?''

"No.''

Lowrie shrugged. "I guess it doesn't make much difference. Let me give you a bit of advice, Harland. There are those who might believe this talk that you killed Lancaster. I wouldn't be at all surprised if you got into trouble by hanging around Edenville.''

"You mean that Lancaster actually had friends?''

"Why wouldn't he?''

"You just told me that the talk says I was hired to kill this Lancaster gent. A friend wouldn't do a thing like that, would he?'' Harland tried to say it easily and naturally. "Who were some of Lancaster's enemies, Lowrie?''

The non-committal look veiled Lowrie's eyes. He rose to his feet. "I trust you understand my position, Harland. I'm a businessman. My business prospers in direct proportion to how much I keep my nose out of people's affairs. I might add that this also applies to you—in regard to the length of your life.''

''Are you making a threat, Lowrie?''

The saloonkeeper displayed that faint smile. ''Making threats is bad for business. I merely made an observation, Harland. Well, I've got to run. I hope you'll enjoy my place.''

With that, Ace Lowrie turned and disappeared into the crowd. Dude stood there a moment longer, his glance insolent and challenging on Harland. Dude's lips were curved in a slight sneer. He seemed to be getting a thrill out of silently baiting Harland. Harland was just going to say something when Dude abruptly left.

Chapter Four

During his first two days in Edenville, Harland just laid around, hoping to pick up some scrap of information about Jim Lancaster. But he had no luck. It seemed that wherever he went he found the same conspiracy of silence so far as Lancaster was concerned. People just clammed up when Harland came around. They were markedly polite to him but they were hardly sociable.

He was tempted more than once these two days to drop the matter. The plan was still half-formed and undecided in his mind. Just exactly what he wanted to do was still not clear to Harland. There was the thought of avenging Lancaster in Harland's brain but he was under no compulsion. After all, Lancaster had chosen to die of his own free will. Had Lancaster wanted to live, he could have dropped Harland with ease. It was the thought of this that chilled Harland.

He was alive only because Lancaster had decided to die. Harland felt he owed something to Lancaster for this.

To ease his mind a little, Harland saddled his bay and rode out of Edenville. He told himself the best thing he could do was to keep riding until he was out of the Stalwarts and then never come back. But he knew he would never do that. He was here to stay until he found what he was looking for—or until he died.

He crossed the valley and rode up into that spur that had branched off from the main mountain range. As he progressed higher he could look down and see the valley and town spread out toy-like below him. He shunned the timber. He stuck to the open spots where he could observe the land both ahead of and behind him. While he had learned nothing about Lancaster during his stay in Edenville, Harland sensed that he had stirred up something. Whoever it was that had wanted Lancaster dead was not glad that Harland had showed up. That much Harland had gathered.

It was during one of these instances when he was scanning his backtrail that Harland spotted the rider. The horseman was far enough away to be unrecognisable. He was just a small black dot, like a bug crawling up the mountain, but he was headed in the direction Harland had taken.

Harland sent the bay ahead and after a quarter of an hour of riding he stopped and looked down the mountain again. The distant horseman came plodding on, following in Harland's wake. Harland cached the bay out of sight and then he lay flat on a rock at the rim of a ledge from where he had a good view of the mountainside. He watched until his eyes ached. The rider came steadily on. There was little doubt in

Harland's mind now that he was being trailed.

Harland rode the bay around the bend and dismounted. Here he was out of sight of anyone coming along his backtrail. To find out who was trailing him, all he had to do was wait.

He leaned his back against the side of the bluff and tried to relax as he waited. He was going to build a smoke, but then he feared that this might give him away and so he just stood there, swallowing hard with an ache that ripped at his throat.

Time dragged on and the rider did not show. Harland began to think that he had been wrong, that the rider had not been trailing him, that he had struck off in another direction.

He was ready to give up in disgust when the sound reached him. It was so faint as to be almost phantasmal, and for the next few instants Harland was positive it was just his imagination playing tricks on him. Then the sound was repeated and this time there was no doubt concerning its actuality. The noise was the metallic ring of a shod hoof striking stone.

The bay perked up its ears, but before the horse could whinny, Harland had clamped his left hand over the bay's muzzle. With his right hand he drew his .44. After the long, dull wait he was eager, even if it meant bloodshed.

Harland waited, hardly daring to breathe. The rider came nearer, his horse moving at a walk. There was the creak of saddle leather in Harland's ears, the mournful jingle of a bit chain. The approaching horse coughed once as if it had swallowed a breath of dust. The sweat of anticipation was pouring down across Harland's eyes when the rider passed the bend into sight.

At first the rider was unaware that Harland was

standing there with his gun in his hand. The horseman rode slumped over a little in weariness, staring down at the tracks that had been laid by Harland's bay. Then the tracks terminated and the rider pulled up with a sharp gasp of surprise. His surprise was not as great as Harland's, however.

Harland froze there in astonishment. The gun suddenly felt heavy and foolish in his hand but he did not put the weapon away. He kept the big bore trained on the rider for a full minute while neither one spoke.

The rider was a woman.

She recovered before Harland. She reined her pinto around until she was facing him and the shock drifted from her face and a small smile curved her mouth.

"You won't make many friends in this country that way, Harland," she said with a trace of amusement in her voice.

Consternation filled Harland. "How do you know my name?" he asked gruffly. He still had not put away his gun.

The woman glanced now at the .44 with an arching of her brows. "You were pointed out to me."

Harland stared at her. Now that the tension had passed from him, he found time to think that she was a very attractive woman. Harland would have put her age in the middle twenties. Even in the saddle she appeared tall for a woman, around five nine or so. Her face, under the wide-brimmed, flat-crowned, black hat, was round and smooth. She was dark and the sun had tanned her skin to a deep brown.

She wore men's clothing. She had on a black and red checkered flannel shirt and over this a blue denim jacket. A blue bandanna was knotted about her throat. She had on blue Levi's that were faded in colour and there was a patch on the left knee. Her plain black boots were scuffed at the toes and her spurs were small, steel, unornamented affairs. Around her waist she had a shell belt and a holstered pistol that to Harland looked like a Bisley .38-40. He glanced long and thoughtfully at this.

He raised his eyes finally and looked at her face and then Harland holstered his .44. She smiled, a little disdainfully, as he put away his weapon but she said nothing. Her eyes regarded him with frank amusement now.

Harland flushed slightly under her study. "Why were you following me?" he asked, lips tight with anger.

Those brows arched again. "What makes you think I was following you?"

"You passed by here, didn't you? I stopped and waited and you caught up with me. You were reading my trail. Why are you following me?"

Her mouth sobered. The humour went out of her eyes. They looked chill and hard now. "I've got a ranch farther ahead," she said, waving an arm. "I'm on my way home."

"I wasn't following any trail," Harland pointed out. "If this is the way to your home, why isn't there a trail or a road?" His eyes narrowed. "You're following me. Why?"

She said nothing. She straightened slowly in the saddle, and, her glance never leaving Harland, she swung a leg back over the cantle of the kak and stepped down to the ground. She stretched to get the stiffness out of herself and Harland saw the thrust of her breasts against her shirt. Then she took two steps towards him and stopped, watching him studiously and soberly now with her head canted a little to one side.

At last she said, "You're right, Harland. I was following you. I want to talk to you."

A wry smile twisted Harland's mouth. "What is there for us to talk about? I don't even know your name."

"My name," she said evenly, "is Mrs. Lancaster. Lorraine Lancaster."

Harland could hear the sibilant sound of his own breathing. For a moment he was stunned, unable to think, unable to do anything but stare in rank disbelief at the woman. Finally he said, "I never knew Lancaster was married."

She held up a hand. "Here is my wedding band," she said, a trifle dryly. "I have the marriage licence at home. Yes, Jim Lancaster and I are legally married."

Harland said nothing.

Her mouth pursed thoughtfully and her eyes were frank as they gazed at Harland. "This is very difficult for me, Harland," she said, her tone rather subdued and with a touch of bewilderment and hesitancy. "I don't know how to begin. I've heard the talk that's gone through the valley." She paused while her eyes studied him. Then she said, "What do you know about my husband, Harland?"

Harland spread his hands. He said nothing. He just could not put anything into words. This was something which he had not expected and it left him feeling helpless and miserable and ashamed.

The woman's face seemed to pale beneath the tan. Her mouth twitched once, spasmodically, and then she said, "I've been told that my husband is dead. Is he, Harland?"

He tried to see if there was grief in her eyes or in her face but she seemed to have drawn a mask over her features. They showed beautiful and cold. If anything, there was a touch of hostility and hate in her glance as she stared at him.

"Have you been told how he was supposed to have died?" Harland asked softly.

"I was told that you killed him."

"Do you believe everything that your hear, Mrs. Lancaster?"

"If I did," she said with a ferocity that chilled the back of Harland's neck, "I wouldn't stand here talking with you. I'd put a bullet in your stinking heart!"

He glanced swiftly and instinctively at the gun in her holster. Her hand rested on her hip just above the handle of the Bisley but her fingers were balled in a fist. She saw his sudden look and she smiled.

"I won't draw on you—this time," she said. "I only want to hear what you have to say." Her brows arched inquisitively. "Well, Harland?"

Harland spread his hands in a helplessness that he felt very strongly. "What can I say?" he told her. "I've heard the same talk you have, Mrs. Lancaster. You know very well that I have a bad rep. I get blamed for lots of things I've never done." He could hear his heart beating loudly again. "Would I have come here to the Stalwarts if I had killed your husband?"

She frowned. She lifted a hand and pulled at her lower lip and those clear blue eyes were slits as she stared at him. "That's what I haven't been able to figure out, Harland. It doesn't make sense to me, your coming here. You must have known that Jim would have friends here. Why have you come, then?"

He shrugged. "I'm just passing through. Isn't this a free country?"

She smiled without humour. "Stop dusting the

trail, Harland. You're here for a reason. What is it?"

"Why do I have to tell you?" he said dryly. "You seem to know more about it than I do."

"You asked a few questions about Jim. You wanted to know if he had any enemies. Why?"

He stared at her with a new interest. "So Lowrie told you."

"Ace Lowrie didn't tell me anything," she snapped. "You did the asking in Ace's saloon. There were other ears listening besides Ace's."

"Whose ears were those?"

She smiled at him jeeringly. "Do you think I'll ever tell you?"

Harland stared at her intently a moment and then he said, "You and me both, Mrs. Lancaster."

"I'm sorry, Harland," she said hurriedly, contritely. She came ahead and laid a hand pleadingly on his arm. Her face turned up a little towards his. "Please, Harland," she said, the hardness gone from her tone now. Her voice quivered and there was anxiety in her glance for the first time. "He's my husband. Don't you see? I've got to know. Either one way or another I've got to know. Won't you tell me, Harland?"

With her close like this, Harland could smell the scent of woodsmoke in her hair and the odour of horse-sweat in her clothing. He was conscious of other things, of her warmth, of the pattern of her breasts beneath the shirt. He stared at the parted mouth while his throat constricted and then a vision of Lancaster's dead face flared across Harland's mind and he recoiled in repulsion.

She did not seem to notice. Her fingers tightened about his arm. "Please tell me, Harland," she begged. "Can't you see how it is for me? I haven't heard from

Jim for a while. There is this talk going around that he's dead. I don't know any more what to do. I love him and I don't know whether he's alive or dead. Don't you see the hell I'm going through, Harland? Won't you help me?''

He could not speak. There was this cold tingling of horror in him and that other thing that made it doubly worse. He shook his head.

She took her hand away and dropped back a step and her head fell as if she were giving up, defeated. But her face lifted in the next instant and the anxiety was gone from it and she was her old calm and insistent self again.

"All right, Harland," she said. "I'll make a deal with you. I can understand why you might not be able to tell me. If Jim is dead and you killed him, I can understand why you don't want to own up to it. So I'll make this deal with you. Even if you killed my Jim, I promise not to do anything about it. Not now, anyway. Later, perhaps, but not now. Even if Jim is dead by your hand I'm giving you my word that I'll just ride off.'' Her eyes were hard and intent on him. "Will you tell me now if my husband is dead, Harland?''

Harland shook his head.

"Maybe you don't believe me, Harland," she said, seeming to get angry. She jerked out the Bisley so swiftly that Harland was caught unaware but she reversed the .38-40 in her hand and extended it to him butt first. "Here, Harland, take my gun. Take it and then tell me.''

Harland shook his head again.

Those blue eyes began to glitter as if with impatience and rage. She punched the shells out of the Bisley and tossed the weapon at Harland's feet. Her voice trembled with suppressed fury when she spoke.

"Do you believe me now, Harland? Do you believe now that I won't do anything to you? You can keep me from getting my gun and even if I do get it, it's unloaded, isn't it? Won't you tell me now? Or don't you believe yet that I'm unarmed? Do you think I've got a hide-out on me? Do you want to search me for one, Harland?"

He shook his head once more. "I'm sorry, Mrs. Lancaster," he murmured. "I don't know anything about your husband."

"You're a dirty liar," she growled in a low, vicious voice. She stepped ahead swiftly and her arm swung, her open hand aiming for Harland's face. But he was not to be caught unawares a second time. He grabbed her arm, twisting it back, harshly and relentlessly, turning her half around with the pressure of it until the pain made her moan. Then he gave a final, swift jerk that ripped a scream out of her and sent her hurtling down on her knees, released from his hold.

He was breathing hard as he stepped back. "Don't ever try to get tough with me again, Mrs. Lancaster," he said. He went over to his bay and mounted. He showed her his back as he rode off, but it was not a dangerous dare. She lay huddled on the ground, weeping softly.

Chapter Five

It was late afternoon when Harland came to the tiny settlement. There was not much to the place. A store, two saloons and a couple of dwellings were huddled together on a small stretch of flat ground. All around the settlement the land rose to merge with the foothills that seemed to crouch here in sullen obeisance to the hulk of the mountain farther ahead.

To Harland's knowledge the place had no name. The reason for its existence was that it was a day's ride from Edenville and therefore provided a limited means of shopping and carousing for those who did not have the time for the ride to Edenville.

Harland pulled up before one of the saloons and dismounted.

A solitary drinker was slouched over the bar at the front end of the room and Harland walked almost to the far end before he stopped. Harland ordered bourbon. He downed his drink instantly and ordered another.

The other customer said, "Give me another one, Art." As the bartender complied, the redhead turned his face so that he stared at Harland. "Will you have one on me, amigo?"

Harland paused. Then he shrugged. The redhead seemed friendly and he looked like he had been drinking and Harland did not want to offend the man. So he said, "Why not, friend?"

The redhead waited until Harland's glass had been filled and then lifted his own shot and said, "Salud," and, throwing his head back, poured the drink into himself with a swift, deft movement. He opened his mouth wide and sighed loudly with pleasure. He began licking his lips in satisfaction while he stared at Harland.

He was a big fellow, standing a couple of inches over six feet and carrying over two hundred pounds on that frame. He had a wide, amiable face and a long mouth that seemed habitually crinkled at the corners in a slight smile. He had huge hands, the backs of them covered with large freckles. His clothes were badly worn, both elbows stuck out of holes in his sleeves. The only well-kept thing about him was the .45 Colt at his right hip.

He belched loudly and went on staring at Harland with that small, happy grin on his mouth. Finally the redhead said, "My name's Antrim. Mitch Antrim."

"Mine's Harland."

The redhead's brows lifted. "So you're Harland?" he said in a tone of wonder. His manner indicated that he had heard of the name and the man. He stared at Harland in frank curiosity but there was nothing offensive about it. There was none of the insolent appraisal or instant dislike and distrust that Harland so often encountered when he announced his identity.

"Well," said the redhead after a short pause, "it's nice knowing you, amigo." He sounded like he meant it.

From outside came the noise of a couple of riders pulling up in front of the saloon. The bartender perked up. He quit staring at the ceiling and began to look happy now that it appeared business was about to pick up. Saddle leather squeaked outside as whoever it was dismounted. Then came the clump of boots, the door was batted open and two men strode into the barroom.

They walked straight up to the middle of the bar without looking to the right or to the left. This indifference was too studied, too deliberate to please Harland. A small tingle laced the back of his neck. He lowered his head and pretended to be toying with his drink, but covertly he appraised the two.

The pair stood at the bar close together and they both ordered whisky. The bartender smiled at them and called one of them Ike and the other one Bronco. He acted like they were good customers of his. However, they were curt with him, merely ordering their drinks and making no comment when the bartender observed that the weather had been pretty good lately.

The one called Ike was a short, heavy-set bull of a man. He had a massive head set on wide, thick shoulders. His barrel chest strained the buttons of his black woollen shirt. He had a paunch but there was nothing soft in appearance about it. It looked hard and formidable. The slanting cartridge belt about his middle was notched for a girth of fifty inches and the plain black holster held a .44 Remington conversion.

Ike's face was wide and square and ugly. Bushy black brows shaded tiny gimlet eyes that seemed sunk deep in their sockets. His nose at one time had been broken and it was still pushed a trifle to one side. The growth of black beard on his face could not quite hide the long, white knife scar on the left cheek. His mouth was always held partly open as if he had difficulty breathing through his nose. His front teeth thus revealed were very white and spaced far apart.

Bronco was tall and cadaverous-looking. It seemed as if he lacked the strength to hold himself up straight, his shoulders were rounded in a perpetual slouch so that his chest was curved inward a little. He moved slowly and even fumblingly, but this was deceptive. A look at his yellow, cat-like eyes belied any notions as to Bronco's harmlessness.

They downed their first round and Ike crooked his finger at the bartender and the glasses were filled up again. The two had not spoken to each other since they had come into the place but, as they raised their glasses for the second time, they looked into each other's eyes and Harland thought they exchanged some secret information. Ike set his shot glass down with an audible thump and sighed loudly.

Ike's back was towards Harland but now Ike turned part way round and swivelled his head still more so that he could look squarely at Harland. Those gimlet eyes seemed to bore into Harland. He felt them taking him apart, weighing him, and then putting him back together again. The glance was heavy and deliberate. Behind Ike, Harland was aware that Bronco, too, was giving him the eye.

Harland lifted his own glance until it locked with Ike's.

"You're a stranger here, aren't you, pal?" Ike asked in a deep rasping voice. "I don't recollect seeing you around before."

Harland gave a short nod.

"You passing right on through or you aiming on hanging around a while?" asked Ike.

Harland shrugged. He said nothing. Inside him, he could feel the sharp, fast thumping of his heart.

The grimace that was supposed to be a smile wavered on Ike's face but he did not let it go out. "I don't mean to be nosy, pal," he said, "but me and my pard are looking for a hand for our place. We've got a spread back there," he said, giving a vague wave of his hand. "Would you like to go to work for us?"

"I'm between jobs," said Harland, "but I'm not yet ready to start looking for my next one."

"We'll pay you good."

Harland's eyes narrowed ever so slightly. "What kind of work you offering?"

"Oh, the usual," said Ike, trying to sound off-hand about it, but Harland sensed a tautness in the man's tone. "Ride fence, hunt strays, work calves. There's not much work right now," he admitted, "but we're looking ahead to round-up time and it's always pretty tough to find hands then because everybody's hiring. So this year we don't aim to be caught short. We'd take you on now just to be set for round-up." His eyes began to glitter. "What do you say, pal?"

"I'm not interested."

"We'll pay good," Ike said again.

"How much do you mean by 'good'?"

"Seventy-five a month and found."

Harland lowered his head a trifle. That old bitterness came flooding back into him and a poignant weariness. This was what he found everywhere. Ike knew him and his rep. There was just one kind of work Ike would have for him.

56

"You and your partner must be doing all right," Harland said wryly. "Most outfits right now are paying thirty, or at best forty. How come you'll go so high? Top hands aren't that scarce."

"They will be when round-up comes."

"I don't think so."

Ike's jaw muscles bulged beneath the black whiskers. He was putting out a visible effort to hold himself in check. "Won't you even ride out to our place for a look-see? It won't cost you nothing."

Harland shook his head. "I'm not interested," he said.

Ike flushed with wrath. His eyes blazed and he spat out an oath. Bronco sauntered across the barroom, passed Ike up and went beyond Harland, too, and stopped only when he came to the wall. Bronco rested his back against the boards and hooked his thumbs in his belt. He was now behind Harland.

Harland turned so that he could observe both Ike and Bronco. There was a glint of triumph in Ike's glance. He gave a swift look about him and saw that the bartender had withdrawn to the other end of the bar, away from involvement in the argument. Antrim was still immersed in his sombre reverie. Ike's eyes swivelled back to Harland.

"You think you're smart, don't you, Harland?" asked Ike.

A chill premonition touched the back of Harland's neck. He was suddenly all wariness. "I thought you didn't know my name," he said flatly.

"I never said so," Ike smirked. His eyes grew mean. "What are you doing in the Stalwarts, Harland?"

"Something that is none of your business!"

Ike started and a harsh growl of anger emitted from

him. "I'm afraid it is our business. If you know what is good for you, you'll tell us, Harland."

Harland looked from Bronco to Ike. They had him good, Harland thought. They had him in a whipsaw and there was not much he could do about it. He could get one of them but he could never hope to get them both. Far back in his mind he began to debate which one it would be.

"I'm looking for some friends of Jim Lancaster," he said softly.

From the corner of his eye, Harland saw Antrim suddenly turn his head and stare at him with a frank interest. Ike sucked in his breath sharply. For a moment he peered hard at Harland as if trying to read his mind. Then Ike displayed that grimacing smile again.

"In that case, Harland, you don't have to look no further. Me and Bronco are damn good friends of Lancaster."

"How can I be sure of that?" asked Harland.

Ike's eyes became glittering pinpoints. "Me and Bronco and Lancaster were in on a business deal." He paused as if to allow this to sink in and then he went on, "That's why you've come to the Stalwarts, isn't it?"

"I'm sick of your questions," Harland growled at Ike. "Run along, bucko."

On the instant Ike's face suffused with rage. Then a cunning and triumphant glint came into his eyes as much as to say that this was what he had planned all along.

"Are you getting tough, Harland?" said Ike with a sneer. "You don't scare me."

"Is that because you've got Bronco with you?"

"Bronco's not in this."

"Then tell him to go outside while you and me have it out. Will you tell him that, Ike?"

Ike growled something unintelligible. His mouth contorted in a brutal grimace of rage. "You've got little choice, Harland," he said. "Me and Bronco want to talk to you in private. Are you coming with us peaceful-like or do we have to carry you?"

"One of you might do the carrying," Harland said grimly, "but it won't be the both of you. One of you is going to be all through in the next minute or so!"

With that, Harland took a step away from the bar and poised his right hand above his .44 He expected to die and he was ready for it.

Harland threw a look at Bronco and saw that the thin man was ready for it but he looked a little shaken in the face of Harland's defiance and apparent fearlessness. Ike was crouched forward, poised on the balls of his feet, his right hand ready to snatch at the handle of his gun. Harland decided it would have to be Ike for he would make the first move, not Bronco. Thus Ike was the more dangerous.

Ike's eyes suddenly flared and Harland told himself, *now!* and grabbed for his .44 when the shot rang out. Ike's hat was lifted from his head and went tumbling to the floor. Bronco's gun was halfway out of its holster but he never finished his draw. Those cat-quick eyes were still for once as they stared fixedly at the other end of the bar.

Ike let go the handle of his gun as if it were red-hot. Snarling with fury, he whipped around and glared at Antrim who stood there, gun in hand. A tiny wisp of smoke was still curling out of the bore of Antrim's .45.

Antrim belched softly and he weaved a little but the gun was rock-steady in his fist. Harland's .44 was in his hand and he covered Bronco with it. Bronco allowed his weapon to slide back in its holster and then he held his hands far out from his side.

"Damn you, Mitch!" Ike shouted, the cords standing out in his neck with rage. "You taking a hand in this?"

"I don't like two hombres ganging up on one," Antrim said quietly. "You know I don't, Ike."

"I'm not forgetting this, Mitch," Ike said darkly.

"Suit yourself," said Antrim, shrugging.

Ike turned back to Harland. For an instant he glared at the gun in Harland's hand. Then his eyes lifted. "We'll meet again, pal," he said quietly. Then Ike summoned Bronco with a jerk of his head and went stamping towards the door, his spurs shrill and angry. They went outside, Ike first, Bronco at his heels. Saddle leather creaked as they mounted.

Harland strolled slowly to the door and Antrim came over beside him. Dusk had come and the bartender finally came out and lighted his lantern. Harland watched Ike and Bronco ride off at a gallop.

"Who are they?" he asked Antrim. Harland's glance was on the two riders disappearing swiftly into the gloom.

"Ike Gibson and Bronco Curtis," said Antrim. "They run a greasy-sack outfit about five miles from here."

Still not looking at Antrim, Harland said softly, "Thanks, amigo."

"That's all right."

Harland turned and looked at Antrim. "Why did you side me?"

"You looked like you needed help. Isn't that reason enough, amigo?"

A smile curved Harland's lips. Antrim was the first

man Harland had met in a long time whom he felt he could like.

"Will you let me buy you a drink?" he asked.

"I never turn down a free one," said Antrim.

They laughed together as they strode back to the bar.

Chapter Six

The next morning Harland rode back to Edenville. Mitch Antrim accompanied him and they reached the town two hours before sundown. Harland returned to his room in the Lamar House. Antrim headed for a saloon. Harland could not get over the feeling that Antrim was despondent about something and this in turn made Harland a little sad, for by now he liked the redhead.

He wondered what connection Ike Gibson and Bronco Curtis had had with Lancaster. He would put nothing past them. They were capable of anything—even the hiring of someone to do away with Lancaster. Harland's eyes turned grim. He would not mind at all if they were what he was looking for.

The last thing Harland experienced before falling asleep was a premonition of utter evil. . . .

He awoke the next morning and after breakfast in

the hotel dining-room he wandered idly about the town. He looked in the various saloons for Mitch Antrim, but the redhead was nowhere to be found. He had undoubtedly left Edenville.

In the afternoon, Harland found a vacant bench in the shady side of the stable and he was sitting there when the rider came up the street and stopped and stared down at Harland. The rider was a youth of about twenty. His horse carried the Bridlebit brand.

"You Dan Harland?" the youth finally asked.

Harland nodded.

"I'm from Bridlebit," the youth said. "My boss, Will Jordan, wants to see you."

"What about?" asked Harland.

The youth shrugged. "He didn't tell me. He just sent me to find you and tell you that if you'll come out to Bridlebit he'll have something interesting to say to you."

Harland's heart had quickened its beat but he did not let on that the news had affected him. "I'll think it over," he said.

"You coming out?" asked the youth.

"Maybe. But not now."

The youth hesitated. "Well, I told you," he muttered after a while as if reassuring himself that he had discharged his duty. He turned his horse around and spurred off at a fast run. Harland watched him go.

They had not delayed in coming to him, Harland thought.

The holdings of Bridlebit lay on the far side of the valley from Edenville and they extended well up into the Stalwarts. Bridlebit was the biggest ranch in the county. Bridlebit owned the most acres and the lushest graze and possessed an abundance of water. The

Jordan family, who owned Bridlebit, were reputed to be very wealthy.

Harland obtained directions on how to reach Bridlebit from the stableman, but he did not leave until early the next morning. Though he was most anxious to find out the reason for his invitation to Bridlebit, Harland decided it was for the best if he did not show himself in too much of a hurry. Then, too, the invitation might not have anything to do with Jim Lancaster. It could concern the matter of hiring out his gun. Harland had received these mysterious invitations before and they had always turned out to be an offer for the use of his gun. The invitation from Bridlebit need not be different.

He reached Bridlebit at noon. The ranch buildings had been built on an eminence. Behind them loomed the massive height of the mountain, green and grey and black and crimson, dwarfing the structures so that they appeared to be puny, fragile, transient things in the face of the mountain's enormousness and indestructibility.

There was an air of prosperity about Bridlebit. The buildings were substantial and well maintained. The sheds and cook shack and bunkhouse had all been given a recent coat of whitewash and so had the corrals. The house was a long, sprawling structure as if whoever had built it had liked a lot of room to move around indoors. The house had been constructed out of stone except for the eaves and the roof.

He passed the blacksmith shop and from within came the ringing clang of iron pounding iron. The bucking bronc squealed in equine rage and someone cursed feelingly. From somewhere out on the range, faint with distance, drifted the bellowing of a bull.

Harland reined in the bay in front of the stone

house as two men came out on the gallery that ran the length of the front of the house. They stood there peering at Harland.

Harland recognised one of them instantly. It was the fancy-dressed gunman he had seen in the Ace of Diamonds, the gunman called Dude Prentiss. Harland frowned. Harland had supposed that Prentiss was Ace Lowrie's bodyguard, yet Prentiss was here at Bridle-bit with that other fellow who could be Will Jordan. A chilly prescience that he could not quite define touched the back of Harland's neck.

When the two on the gallery saw that Harland made no move to dismount, they stepped down on the ground and walked up to him.

Prentiss's companion appeared to be a year or two younger than Harland. This fellow was burly-chested and he had wide shoulders and he was carrying the beginnings of a paunch. He was bareheaded and his blond hair seemed to gleam in the sun. His face was pleasant but the receding chin and the soft jowls betokened a weakness in him and a proclivity for soft living. His clothes were plain but of a cut better than those of an ordinary working man. He did not wear a gun.

Prentiss stayed a step behind the blond fellow. Those fancy spurs of Prentiss's jingled musically as he walked. They came up to Harland and stopped and the blond fellow said:

"Are you Harland?"

Harland nodded.

"I'm Will Jordan," said the fellow. "Won't you dismount, Harland? We can talk down by that corral." He indicated the place with a nod of his head.

Harland stepped to the ground. He glanced at Prentiss. "What does he have to do with this?" Harland asked Jordan.

Jordan looked uncomfortable. "Dude's a friend of mine."

"Is he connected with what you have to tell me?"

For the moment, Jordan seemed bewildered. He shot a quick look at Prentiss as if for guidance, then hurriedly shifted his eyes. "Uh—no," he said.

"Then tell Prentiss to stay here." Harland paused, then he said, "He can watch us from here—in case you're scared of something, Jordan."

"What would I be scared of?" Jordan snapped. Then he looked flustered again. "Better stay here, Dude," he mumbled and, with his eyes studying the ground, he led the way to the corral.

When they got there he said, "I—I don't know how to begin."

"There are only two things you'd want to discuss with me, Jordan," Harland said quietly. "Either the hiring of my gun—or Jim Lancaster. Which is it?"

"I'm not interested in your gun. It's—I've got something about Lancaster to tell you."

"What about him?"

Jordan started to sweat.

"What are you scared of?" Harland asked.

"I'm not—all right, Harland, I am scared. I'm scared of you."

"Me?" said Harland, astounded. "Why are you scared of me?"

Jordan's eyes were luminous with fear. "It's what I'm going to tell you about Lancaster." He made a pathetic gesture with his hands. "I'm not packing a gun, Harland."

"I can see that. Go on and tell me, Jordan. I won't hurt you."

"You've been trying to find out who wanted Lancaster dead. It was me, Harland. I hired Buckskin Tom Elliott to hire someone to get Lancaster for me."

"Why should you want Lancaster dead?" Harland finally asked.

Jordan shot another glance up at Prentiss. The Dude had not stirred. He stood there with both thumbs hooked in his shell belt. His gaze never strayed from Harland.

"He was giving me trouble," said Jordan. He seemed recovered from most of his dread. His tone was no longer strained. "Lancaster was running off my cows. I warned him but he wouldn't stop. So—I had him killed."

"That's pretty drastic, isn't it?" said Harland wryly. "Why didn't you sign a complaint and let the law handle him?"

"Lancaster was too slick. I couldn't get any proof that would stand up in court. I had no choice, Harland. I had to protect my property. I figured if Lancaster was taken care of, that would discourage anybody else who might get ideas of running off Bridlebit stock." Jordan paused and stared intently at Harland. "You believe me, don't you, Harland?" He sounded like he was begging.

Harland jerked a thumb at Prentiss. "Where does he come into this?" he asked Jordan.

"Dude's a friend of mine."

"People are liable to get the wrong idea about you, Jordan," he said, "when a man like Dude keeps hanging around."

Jordan flushed and ducked his head. "He's just a friend," he mumbled.

"Maybe," said Harland. He started walking up to his horse.

Jordan came after him, full of anxiety. "I told you everything there is to know about Lancaster. You wanted to know who was really after him, didn't you? Well, I told you, didn't I? You believed me, didn't you?"

"Sure, I believed you," said Harland.

Prentiss was standing by the bay but Harland scarcely gave the Dude a glance. He could hardly wait to get away. He could no longer endure Will Jordan's pitiful efforts at being convincing.

"Well, that's the way it was, Harland," Jordan was saying as Harland mounted. "I had to have Lancaster killed. He was running off Bridlebit stock, don't you see? I couldn't stand it any more. I—"

"Shut up, Will," snapped Prentiss.

"But Dude. I was just telling Harland why—"

"Shut up," Prentiss said again.

In the saddle, Harland laid a cold, calculating look on Prentiss. He touched the bay with the spurs and rode off. His back flinched for a while, but nothing happened, and by the time he had passed out of the ranch yard, Harland was breathing again. . . .

He rode without hurry. Sunlight was warm and lazy and the valley about him was green with graze and he wasn't going anywhere in particular, so he took his time. He could feel the pull of it in his heart, the pull of this other life he had once known, and the sensation left him filled with a gentle sadness. He was not one to moan about it, however, and he dismissed it from him with a nettled curse.

He topped a small rise and reined in the bay. Some distance away a small herd of white-faces were grazing. Harland folded his forearms across the saddlehorn and watched the cows a while.

How long he was absorbed like this Harland did

not know. He was jerked out of it by the sound of a running horse and he looked up to see a rider racing up to him. The horse was a palomino, a picture animal, and for the instant Harland's attention was fixed by the horse. When he finally lifted his glance he saw that the rider was a girl.

She reined in the palomino about five feet away and she sat there in her fancy, white-trimmed saddle, breathing a little hard from the exertions of her fast ride and watching Harland out of narrow-lidded eyes. She looked to be about twenty. Her golden blonde hair under the cream-coloured Stetson reached down to brush against her shoulders. Her face was small and round and tanned lightly by the sun. She had long, thin, black brows and intent grey eyes.

She was dressed plainly but expensively. The white blouse was open in front enough to reveal the first white rise of her breasts. She was wearing a buckskin jacket and a buckskin divided riding skirt. Her boots had a lot of white stitching and her small-rowelled spurs were plated with silver. From her right wrist dangled a quirt.

Harland stared at her, thinking that she was just about the most beautiful girl he had ever seen. There seemed to be something familiar about her but he just couldn't place it.

There was nothing friendly in the way the girl looked at him. After a full minute of watching him, she said, "What did you want with my brother?"

"Who is your brother?" he said.

"Don't give me that," she snapped. Then she seemed to think it over and she said, a trifle less hostilely, "I'm Glennis Jordan."

Harland nodded and touched the brim of his hat. He said nothing.

"You're Dan Harland, aren't you?" asked Glennis Jordan.

"That's right."

"What did you want with my brother?"

Harland remembered Will Jordan's apprehensive glance up at the house. This girl must be the reason for it. "Well, now, Miss Jordan," drawled Harland, "shouldn't your brother be the one to tell you that?"

She coloured a little and this display seemed to make her angrier. "I'm not asking my brother," she said stiffly. "I'm asking you, Harland."

He began to feel irritated at her manner. "Have you ever heard of confidential information, Miss Jordan? I've never been one to run off at the mouth."

"Then you refuse to tell me?"

"That's right."

She appeared to be struggling hard to keep a hold on her temper. "I've heard of you, Harland," she said, her voice quivering with the control she imposed on it. "You're a gunfighter, a trouble-maker. I want you to stay away from my brother."

"Isn't he old enough to look after himself?" asked Harland. "He should be the one running this outfit, not the other way around."

"Why, you impudent—" she began angrily. She spurred the palomino suddenly, hurtling the animal towards Harland, and her right wrist, holding the quirt, rose high. The instant the palomino moved, Harland jabbed his spurs home. The bay lunged to meet the palomino and the two horses collided. Harland reached out swiftly, grabbing the girl's arm before she could swing the quirt at him. He squeezed her wrist hard until she moaned with pain.

"You so much as touch me with that quirt, miss," Harland said through his teeth, "and I'll use it on you right where you sit down.'' He gave a sharp jerk to her arm that wrenched a gasp of pain out of her. His mind was full of a rolling anger. ''Now you listen to me,'' he growled. ''I didn't come to Bridlebit. I was sent for. I never laid eyes on your brother until a short while ago. He'll get no trouble from me unless he comes asking for it. Is that clear? If you want to know what we talked about, ask him. If he wants to tell you, it's all right with me, but you're not getting a single word out of me. Is that clear?''

He released her and reined the bay away. She lowered her head and turned her face away from him. He thought he heard her sob once.

After a few moments, she regained her composure. She made a furtive dab at her eyes and then she straightened in her saddle and faced Harland, again haughty and defiant.

''Stay away from Bridlebit,'' she told him in that cold and distant tone, ''and leave my brother alone. Understand?''

Reining the palomino around sharply, she brushed him with her spurs and sent him away at a swift, drumming run. Her long hair fanned out behind her in the breeze raised by the horse's speed. Harland watched until she was out of sight.

He felt very shallow inside.

Chapter Seven

The man sat in the lobby of the Lamar House, watching Harland as he came in through the door. Harland was instantly aware of the fellow's interest in him and he darted a quick look that way.

The man sat with his chair tilted back against the wall. It was around supper-time and the fellow must have just come from the dining-room. He had sharpened the end of a match and he was using this to pick his teeth and he kept sucking loudly to help dislodge some stubbornly stuck food particles. His eyes caught Harland as he came in the lobby and then the glance never left him.

He made no secret of his interest in Harland and this riled Harland a little. However, he was tired from his ride out to Bridlebit and back and so he ignored the fellow and went up to his room. After he washed and changed, Harland came downstairs. The man still sat in the lobby and once more his glance took up Harland and followed him as he went into the dining-room.

Harland took his time with his supper. When he was through, he went back to the lobby and saw that the man in the brown suit was still tilted back in his chair. He must have cleaned his teeth to his satisfaction for now he had the match-stick clamped in his mouth while both thumbs were hooked in pockets of his vest. His eyes picked up Harland the instant he stepped into the lobby.

Harland walked over to the fellow and stopped and looked down at him. "What's so interesting about me, bucko?" he asked quietly.

"You look like someone I knew once," the man in the brown suit said blandly. "Back on the Brazos I think it was. Or maybe up in the Panhandle. You ever been in those parts, cowboy?"

"Never," said Harland.

"My mistake," the man in brown murmured. "Sorry, cowboy."

Harland kept his look on the man a moment longer; then he turned away and went outside. As he passed through the door, he could feel those eyes on his back.

He wandered over to the Ace of Diamonds and had a couple of drinks. He spotted Ace Lowrie, but the saloon-keeper just nodded at Harland and made no attempt at conversation. Dude Prentiss did not appear to be in the barroom. Rose came downstairs and spied Harland and started for him. He decided now was a good time to leave, and before she was halfway to the bar Harland was on his way outside. Behind him he heard Rose use a very unladylike expression.

He stepped outside, feeling relaxed and at peace with the world. The turmoil he had been through these recent days seemed far away and unreal to him at this moment. It was almost like those long-gone days before he had taken up the way of the gun. He paused just outside and filled his lungs with a deep breath of air and it was just at this instant that the bore of the six-shooter was shoved against Harland's back.

It was done so silently and skilfully and swiftly that Harland was not aware of it until the gun made contact. Belatedly, he started a pass at his own .44 but he checked himself before his hand had touched his gun handle. The next instant he felt his .44 being lifted from its holster.

Harland's heart was pounding rapidly. He wanted to turn to see who it was, but the six-shooter kept bearing down hard against his back and the lack of anything being said impressed Harland that he was up against someone who knew what he was about. Harland was holding his hands slightly out from his side and suddenly there was the cold snap of steel about one wrist and before he could fight it that arm had been pulled behind him and manacled to his other. It was accomplished with a deftness that implied much practice at this sort of thing.

Now the gun finally eased its pressure. Harland turned. Facing him, gun in hand, was the man who had been watching him in the hotel.

The man said, "Let's go to Beeson's stable, Harland."

"What is this?" demanded Harland.

With his left hand, the man turned back the lapel of his coat. In the lamplight spilling out of the Trail Bar, Harland caught a glimpse of a badge pinned beneath the lapel. He could not make out what kind of badge it was.

"What's the charge?" asked Harland. He did not move.

"Let's go to Beeson's," the man said in a hard, uncompromising way. "You'll get the details later, Harland. Right now we're going for a little ride."

"Where to?"

"To the county seat at Apache Springs." The man gestured slightly with his six-shooter. "Get a move on, cowboy."

"What about my things at the Lamar House?" asked Harland.

"They'll be sent to you." The six-shooter waggled again. "Move, cowboy."

They rode north from Edenville for about an hour and then the man in the brown suit turned west and in a short while they were climbing that spur that had branched off from the main range of the Stalwarts. Harland recalled his experiences of a few days ago in this part of the mountain. He remembered Lorraine Lancaster, poignantly, and also Ike Gibson and Bronco Curtis—and Mitch Antrim.

He began to wonder if the man in the brown suit were in the employ of one of these, but when morning came, Harland saw that they were not on the way to the tiny settlement where he'd had his run-in with Ike Gibson and his partner. Harland had never seen this part of the Stalwarts. They were up rather high and ahead of them was a notch in the backbone of the mountain and they appeared to be heading for this.

They stopped to rest their horses and Harland tried questioning his captor. The man in the brown suit did not say a word. Rage rose in Harland and he stormed and raved, but the man in brown remained adamant and silent. When Harland became convinced that he could accomplish nothing, he lapsed into sullen silence.

Two hours later they reached the notch and passed through it and now they seemed to be in another world. This side of the mountain was entirely different from the lush greenness of the opposite slopes. This side was barren and desolate. Isolated pines grew here and there and the ground had little graze, mostly only sagebrush, and the sun seemed to have a hellish wickedness as it glared down.

They rode for another hour and in that time Harland saw no sign of any living thing except for a vulture that wheeled and banked high in the burnished sky above them. At the end of the hour they came to the first sign that anyone had ever been hardy enough or foolish enough to challenge the unrelenting harshness of this land.

The ranch had been long abandoned. The roof of the house had caved in and a strong wind in the past had bowled over one of the sheds. There were two corrals and in both of them the fence rails were broken in places so that the corrals could no longer contain any animals. This ranch was as desolate and hopeless a ruin as Harland had ever seen.

The man in brown led the way into one of the corrals in which a snubbing post still thrust up out of the ground. Near the post the man dismounted. He untied the rope that bound Harland's legs underneath his bay and then he spoke.

"Get off your horse, Harland."

Harland was so weak and stiff that he could hardly stand for he had not been out of the saddle since they had left Edenville. He had no strength to resist while the man in brown dropped a loop over him, tightening it about his chest, and then pulled him up against the snubbing post and tied him there.

Harland said angrily, "What the hell is going on? I thought you were taking me to Apache Springs. Who are you and what are you trying to do?"

The man smiled with little humour. "Hold your horses, Harland. I'll be getting down to business pronto. First, you better have a drink of water."

He held the canteen while Harland drank. Then the man set the canteen down on the ground. He said, "This is the last drink you're going to have, Harland, until you've answered me a few questions." He drew a deep breath. "My name is Cal Worthington. I'm an investigator for the Border Pacific Railroad. I am here to find out who held up that B.P. pay car at Conestoga Pass last June seventeenth and what has happened to the hundred thousand dollars that was stolen from it."

"June seventeenth?" echoed Harland. "I was nowhere in the Stalwarts at the time, and I can prove it."

"I've no doubt about that," said Worthington, showing that slight, humourless smile again. "What I want to learn from you, Harland, is this. Where is the hundred thousand?"

Harland peered through narrowed eyes at Worthington. "Are you crazy?" Harland asked. "How can I know where the money is when I wasn't even in on the hold-up?"

Again Worthington displayed the thin, taut smile. His eyes, behind his spectacles, glittered with firmly controlled rage. "I am not going to argue with you, Harland," he said quietly. "To keep you from asking what this is all about, I am going to give you the details, so you will no longer have any excuse to pretend ignorance."

He paused as if he were going over in his mind what he planned to say. "The night of June seventeenth," Worthington began, "the Border Pacific pay car was held up in Conestoga Pass by three men. I have a pretty good idea who the three were—Ike Gibson, Bronco Curtis and Jim Lancaster. I have no proof yet that will be acceptable in a court of law, but I am pretty sure they are the bandits. For the present, I am not so much interested in arresting the bandits as I am in recovering the money. A hundred thousand dollars is a lot of dinero," he said musingly.

"I still don't see where I come into it," Harland said.

"I'm coming to that," said Worthington. "The hold-up came off slick as a whistle. Then the three bandits had a falling out. Lancaster got the idea of pulling a double-cross and keeping all the money himself. He did that and skipped the country. That's where you come in, Harland."

Harland could hear the solid thumping of his heart. "I still don't see how you can connect me with the hold-up or the money, Worthington."

"You killed Jim Lancaster, didn't you?"

"Since you know so much about it, why don't you tell me?"

"That is just what I am going to do, Harland," snapped Worthington. His hands trembled with rage and he closed his fists and then shoved his hands in his pockets. "You came to the Stalwarts for a very good reason. You came for that hundred thousand dollars!"

The shock of it stunned Harland for a moment. "That's the craziest thing I ever heard, Worthington."

"It's a crazy world we're living in, Harland." His

eyes behind the spectacles were slits. "Somehow, you learned from Lancaster before he died where he cached the money. The railroad wants that money back, Harland. They want the money even more than the criminals. Where is it, Harland?"

Sweat was streaming down Harland's face. "If I knew where the money was, Worthington, why haven't I picked it up and left? Why have I hung around the Stalwarts? You don't make sense."

"You haven't had a chance to pick it up, that's why," said Worthington. "You've been watched and trailed ever since you came here and you've been aware of it and so you've let the money lay. You're just waiting for the day when no one will be after you. That is when you plan to grab the money and leave. Well, that day isn't going to come, Harland," he said softly. "You're going to tell me where to find that money. You're going to tell me now."

Harland shook his head helplessly. "You've got it all wrong, Worthington. It isn't at all the way you've got it figured out."

"Tell me, Harland." Worthington said it with deceptive gentleness.

"How can I tell you when I've got no idea where it is?"

"All right," said Worthington. He sounded very mild. He reached down and picked up the canteen at his feet. He held the canteen in front of Harland's eyes and shook it so that Harland could hear the water sloshing around inside. Worthington's glance was cold and relentless.

"You're not getting anything to drink, Harland," he said quietly. "You're not getting anything to eat. You're staying tied to that post until you tell me."

With that, Worthington turned on his heel and

strode off. The last sound Harland heard was the swishing of the water in the canteen.

Then hell began for Harland. At first it wasn't too bad, and he actually deceived himself that he could endure it. The sun was hot on him. It was now directly overhead and it beat down on him but it was not something that he could not resist. It was the rope, wound round and round him, binding him to the snubbing post, that bothered him the most. He was tired, his legs could hardly support him, but when he allowed himself to sag against the ropes, they cut into his body with an excruciating insistence and he had to force his weight back on his weary legs once more. That was at the beginning, while his body still contained a fair amount of moisture.

It was when he began to feel the sun that the torment rose to a pitch he could not believe possible, except that he was experiencing it and thus he knew it was so. He tried to move around the post to put his back to the sun, but he was too securely tied and he could not budge. The best he could do was lower his head and avert his face as much as he could away from the sun's ruthless glare. But, after a while, the cramps started to pinch and squeeze the cords of his neck and he had to turn his face around and endure the agony of the sun the best he could.

Then Worthington came back. In his right hand he held a canteen. With a deliberate, exaggerated slowness, he unscrewed the cap and then lifted the canteen to his lips. He drank with great, avid, gulping swallows, and he was careless so that some of the water flowed over his lips and down across his chin from where it fell, dripping, to the ground. When he was through drinking, he uttered a loud sigh of pleasure and wiped his mouth and chin with the back of a hand. He put the cap back on the canteen and then shook it so that Harland could hear the maddening slosh of the liquid inside.

"Are you ready to tell me, Harland?" Worthington asked.

"I can't," Harland croaked.

"You'll get a drink of water if you tell me."

"I don't know," groaned Harland.

"All right," said Worthington, "you're the one who's got it tough. I don't mind waiting." He walked away.

Harland looked forward to evening. As the sun went down, Harland prayed to hurry it along. He almost wept with eagerness thinking of the moment when its heat would no longer torment him. But when darkness came, he found it was just as bad as the boiling hellishness of the day.

With the death of the day a driving chill took over the air. It did not seem possible after the oven-like heat of the afternoon that such a precipitate change in temperature could occur. Yet Harland felt the cold's needle-like persistence as it probed at his flesh.

Up by the ruins of the house, Worthington had a fire going. Its flames leaped and shimmered against the black of the night and Harland gazed at the fire with great longing. At one time he was tempted to cry with despair, but he averted his glance and gnashed his teeth instead. He would have cursed except that his throat was too parched.

Harland lost all track of time. Finally, in utter exhaustion he dozed off.

The first half hour after sunrise was the best of all as the chill of night departed and the air grew grati-

fyingly warm. The sun seemed generous and its first
rays were a blessing rather than a curse. Then it got
up higher and abruptly it shook off its lethargy and
got down to work again, making the air a stifling,
burning hell about Harland.

Worthington came, carrying a coffee-pot in one
hand, and the aroma of the hot coffee hit Harland's
nostrils and he thought he would retch from the longing and the pain in his empty stomach. He made no
effort to ask Worthington for some; he knew it was
useless to beg. Worthington's heart was as unfeeling
as a chunk of stone ripped out of the bowels of the
mountain.

Worthington stared at Harland a long time. Finally,
Worthington said, "I'm listening, Harland."

Harland said nothing. His throat was too full of
anguish to try to speak and if he did speak Worthington would not believe him. So Harland remained silent and stared down at the swimming ground.

Worthington peered intently at Harland's downcast
head. "Can you hear me, Harland?" he asked. When
Harland did not speak and failed to move, Worthington came ahead and pushed up Harland's face as if
checking to see if Harland were unconscious—or
dead.

With Worthington's face only inches away, Harland tried to spit at it, but his mouth and throat were
too dry for him to work up even the tiniest bit of
spittle. Worthington stepped back hastily, the corners
of his mouth twitching with anger.

Worthington's spartan self-control finally snapped.
His eyes glared madly and his voice rose to a screech.
"Tell me, damn you, Harland, tell me! Do you want
to hang to the post until you die? I'll do it. I promise
you, Harland, I'll do it! If you don't tell me, I'll let

you hang there until you rot and the vultures pick your bones clean!''

Then, just as suddenly as he'd lost his head, Worthington had himself in hand again. His voice became soft and solicitous. ''Let's be reasonable about it, Harland. I don't like being cruel. Look. I've got some coffee here. How about you telling me where that hundred thousand is cached and then I'll untie you and we'll sit down and drink coffee together and eat some fatback and biscuits that I've got up at the fire. What do you say?''

Harland did not speak. He just hung there listlessly, his arms and legs numb with pain, his chest bulging with pain, his eyes streaked with pain, his brain shrieking with pain. He no longer cared if he lived or died.

''I'll tell you what I'll do,'' said Worthington. ''I don't blame you for wanting to hang on to that money, Harland, but what good will it be to you? The railroad will know that you have it and you'll be hunted. You'll have to live in hiding, and what kind of life is that? Look. This is what I'll do. You turn the money over to me and I'll talk to the railroad about you. The B.P. will be happy and grateful to have all that money back and they'll reward you, Harland. It won't be as large a sum as you have now, naturally, but it will be all yours and you'll be a free man and able to come and go as you please. Now isn't that fair, Harland?''

Harland said nothing. The ground kept reeling and lurching in his gaze and so he shut his eyes, but then it seemed that his body was caught in a raging vortex that whirled and hurled him through dizzying immensities of space.

''I'm trying very hard not to lose my temper,'' said

Worthington, his voice edged and tight. "I'm trying very hard to be humane. I don't want to be brutal with you, Harland, but if you give me no choice—"

At this instant there was an explosion and Worthington cried out in alarm. Harland's eyes batted open. The explosion came again and it seemed to Harland that it had sounded like a gunshot. He blinked his eyes and tried to shake the fuzziness from his brain and his eyes finally began to clear a little. The world still rocked somewhat in his sight but he could discern what was going on.

Worthington had retreated off to one side. His hands were raised and he was hatless, his white hair glinting like silver in the sun. Another shot cracked out, kicking dirt over Worthington's toes, and then the voice came:

"Drop your gunbelt, pop, and then cut those ropes and take those cuffs off Harland. You better not try anything funny, either. I didn't shoot that hat off your head by accident."

Harland turned his gaze in the direction of the voice and at first he thought his eyes were still playing tricks on him. But stare hard as he would the image would not change and he knew it to be real.

Just inside the corral, smoking Bisley in hand, stood Lorraine Lancaster.

Chapter Eight

The Quarter Circle L Ranch lay rather high up in the Stalwarts. It lay on the lush side of the mountain, but already this far up the graze was thinning out and the timber was not as tall and majestic as it was lower on the mountain. The buildings of Quarter Circle L were few and unprepossessing. The house was a small, two-room affair built out of rough, unpeeled pine logs. There was also a small barn built in the same fashion. The two corrals were not too large and were connected by a chute. Quarter Circle L had belonged to Jim Lancaster.

His first night there, Harland hardly realised where he was. His body and mind were still a torment of agony to him and the events of the two preceding days and nights pinwheeled and paraded crazily and disorderly through his brain. He cried out loudly now and then, unaware that he was doing so. He flung the smothering blankets off his quivering body as he felt the scorching of the sun again. And other times, though covered with several blankets, his teeth chattered as his body was ravaged by a savage chill. He babbled and laughed and cried.

He awoke with the sun in his eyes and he lay there quietly for a while, trying to figure out where he was. He was alone in this room. When he tried to roll over on his back his body protested with streaks of shrieking pain, but he finally managed it. As he lay there, the jumbled events straightened out in his mind and clear recollection came.

Thinking about it brought a great weariness to Harland and he turned his face towards the wall and was just beginning to doze again when he heard someone enter the room. He opened his eyes and turned his head and saw Lorraine Lancaster.

She stopped just inside the door when she saw that he was awake. She stared at him a while. Then she said, "I see you've come out of it." She sounded neither friendly nor hostile. There was a grave look on her face. Those light blue eyes looked strangely luminous against the darkness of her face.

She stared soberly down at Harland. "Would you like a little broth, Harland?" she asked.

He nodded. He watched her as she walked away. He did not like what he was beginning to feel inside. . . .

She propped him up with pillows and then fed him the broth with a spoon. She sat on the edge of the bed and Harland was very aware of her nearness. He felt his throat constrict a couple of times so that he could hardly swallow, and in the same instant that he was conscious of her proximity he wished that she would go away. Every now and then Harland saw the dead face of Jim Lancaster.

When Harland had finished the broth, she left the room. He felt rather sad and lonely now that she was gone. . . .

Harland slept again and when he awoke he felt refreshed. He figured it was afternoon and he decided it was time he got out of here. He swung his legs over the edge of the bed and sat up, and the pain of it made him think he was going to pass out. But it let up enough for him to begin dressing. His shirt and trousers were draped over the back of a chair and his shell belt and holstered .44 were also hung there. His boots were beside the chair.

A couple of times he thought he was going to faint, but he got his shirt and trousers on. Then he sat on the edge of the bed to begin putting on his boots when Lorraine Lancaster entered.

She stared at him in surprise and said, "Where do you think you're going?"

"About my business," said Harland.

She watched him wince as he bent over with a boot. "You can stay here for another day or so," she said. "I won't charge you for it if that's what you're afraid of."

Harland flushed. "Thanks for everything," he said. He could not bend over enough to pull on the boot and the pain of the effort took his wind away so that he gave it up for the moment and straightened.

She was watching him intently. "You won't get very far the condition you're in," she said. "You had a rough deal. You need more rest."

"How did you find me?" he said.

"I was looking for strays. Once in a while a few of them wander up through the notch to the other side of the mountain. I saw the smoke of Worthington's fire and when I rode up, there you were.''

He said ''Thanks'' again and picked up a boot once more. He felt miserable and ill at ease. He had killed her husband and she had rescued him from Worthington. Just how he could discharge this obligation which he felt so strongly Harland did not know. He wanted to get away from this place and especially this room which had been slept in by her and Lancaster.

But he could not get the boot on this time, either.

She said, ''I could put your boots on for you, Harland, but I'm not going to. You can try to leave and I won't stop you, but I won't rope your horse for you and I won't saddle him for you. You'll just have to get along by yourself.''

She left the room then. Sweat was dripping down Harland's face. He knew he was in no condition to ride. He thought longingly of another night's rest in a good bed and he realised now that as much as he wanted to leave, he also wanted to stay.

He dropped the boot to the floor and sank down on his back on the bed. He tried not to think of what was in his mind. He felt all rotten inside.

For supper, she brought him beefsteak and potatoes and fresh biscuits and coffee and some apple pie she had baked that afternoon. He sat on the edge of the bed and wolfed all the food down. She sat in the chair, watching him eat. Once when he glanced at her, she caught his eye and held it a moment, then averted her gaze while a flush crept over her face. Neither one of them spoke. When Harland was through, she carried the emptied dishes out of the room. Harland waited, but she did not return. He knew he should be glad, but his heart did not feel that way. He kept seeing her before his eyes all the time.

He was beginning to get some idea of the kind of man Jim Lancaster had been. Harland had discounted Will Jordan's story about Lancaster being a rustler. That story had obviously been fabricated, but for what reason Harland could not guess. However, he believed Cal Worthington's account of the Border Pacific robbery. There was no doubt in Harland's mind that Lancaster had participated in the holdup, but whether Lancaster had been an out-and-out tough and outlaw or whether he had been inveigled into the stick-up Harland could not decide.

The early part of the evening Harland could hear the woman moving about in the next room, but she never showed herself. She did not come in once to see how he was. After darkness had come, there was only silence beyond Harland's door and he supposed that she was sleeping somewhere there. He waited a long while for drowsiness to come to him, he waited with all those random images and recollections parading in front of his eyes. He began to think that this night he was never going to drop off but, eventually, he slept, restlessly, but still he slept.

He awoke, and the first thing he realised was that the morning was well on its way. The sun came slanting in through the window, laying a small golden rectangle on the floor, and somewhere outside a horse nickered. He thought it sounded like his bay.

He found that he was not so stiff this morning and that most of the soreness was gone from his body. He had no difficulty in dressing, and by the time he was through the little stiffness that had been left in him was completely gone. He strapped on his belt and gun and then walked out of the room.

He had started for the corral in which he had spotted his bay when Lorraine came outside and called his name. "Don't you want anything to eat before you go, Harland?" she asked.

He stopped in his tracks but he did not turn to face her. "I've bothered you enough already," he said.

"Nonsense," she declared. "I've got coffee on and the flapjack batter ready. It won't take but a few minutes to get your breakfast ready."

He turned back reluctantly, yet deep within him there was an eagerness. "All right," he said, not meeting her eyes.

He ate in silence, not looking at her, but conscious all the while of her gaze on him. He was uncomfortable and felt relieved when he was through and rose from the table. He gave her a fleeting glance and thanked her and then went out of the door.

As he started for the corral, he became aware that she was following him. His saddle had been thrown across the top pole of the corral and he took his kak down and saw that she had come up beside him.

He looked at her. There was that graveness about her lips, and something seemed to be haunting the depths of those light blue eyes.

"I don't want you to get the idea, Harland," she said, "that I'm asking for anything in return for what I've done for you. I would have done as much for any stranger that I'd have found in the spot you were in. You don't have to do anything for me, Harland." She took a deep breath. "But I would like to know about my husband."

"I can't tell you, Mrs. Lancaster."

"Why can't you?"

He shook his head numbly and started to turn away. Her fingers tightened about his arm; they dug into his flesh. "Look at me, Harland," she said. "Why can't you tell me?"

He stopped with his back to her. He stood there silent.

"Is it because you killed him?" she asked. "Is that why you can't tell me?"

"I don't want to say a thing about it."

"I promised you once, Harland, and I'll promise you again, if you've killed him and you'll tell me, I promise not to do anything about it. Not for a while, anyway. Don't you believe me, Harland?"

"I believe you," he said sadly.

"Then why don't you tell me?"

He shrugged. He was tired of holding the saddle and he placed it on the ground, but he did not turn to face her.

She was quiet for a while, as if she were going over something in her mind. Finally she said, "What if I were to tell you I don't think you killed my husband? What if I were to tell you I think he's still alive? What would you say to that, Harland?"

He turned now and stared at her. Her face looked troubled and sad, but there was something deep in her eyes which he could not fathom. It left him uneasy and suspicious.

"You don't believe me, do you?" she said when Harland did not speak. "Well, I just can't convince myself that you'd kill Jim and then come here where Jim has friends. There is such a thing as vengeance, Harland, and you know it." Her eyes narrowed now. "Who sent you here, Harland? Why are you trying to find out things about my husband? If you want to know something about him, why don't you ask me?"

91

"All right," said Harland, his face grim. "I'll ask you. Did your husband have any enemies?"

"I suppose all of us have people who don't like us."

"Is there anyone around here who disliked your husband enough to want him dead?"

She cocked her head to one side and stared at him. The colour drained from her features and her lips were almost white. "Why do you want to know that, Harland?"

He ignored her query. "Is there someone around here like that, Mrs. Lancaster?"

"Not that I know of."

He drew a deep breath. "What do you know about Cal Worthington?"

"I know who he is and why he's here."

"Was your husband in that stick-up?"

She drew back a step and her eyes seemed to glitter as she looked at him and the corners of her mouth pinched. "Is that why you're here?" she asked suddenly. "Are you after the money?"

"I didn't know about the stick-up or the money until Worthington told me."

"Then why are you here? Who sent you, Harland?"

"I won't answer that."

"Harland," she said. She paused a moment, then plunged on. "Jim and I were married for five years. I won't say they were bad years or especially happy years. We were married and that was that and we tried to make the best of it. Jim was restless and unhappy with what he had. We started this ranch up here, but you can see this isn't land like they've got down in the valley. We scratched out a living and that was all. It started getting on Jim's nerves. He wanted progress, he wanted something to show for his work. I guess that's why he helped stick up that train. He wanted his pile and he wanted it quick.''

He could feel her eyes probing his face. ''Can't you see what I'm trying to tell you, Harland?'' she said, her voice almost a whisper.

With her face turned up like that and close to his, he could feel the warmth of her breath on his lips. Suddenly, he did not care to fight it any more. The right or wrong of it no longer mattered to him. What he felt in his heart and mind transcended all other considerations, and he reached out and pulled her roughly and hungrily against him and bruised his lips down on hers.

There was nothing inhibitive or reluctant about her, and he held her crushingly while all other sensations fled from his mind and he knew only sweetness and desirability and an overwhelming yearning.

''Is it awful of me to feel this way?'' she asked him. ''Are you ashamed of me, Harland? I know I should hate you and want to kill you if you've killed Jim, but I can't feel that way any more. Do you understand, Harland?''

He nodded.

''Do you feel the same way about me, Harland?''

''I've always felt that way about you, Lorraine.''

''What will we do, Harland?''

''I don't know.''

''I've got to know how I stand.''

''What do you mean?''

''Am I married—or am I a widow?''

He stared gravely down at her tear-stained face. ''Someday I'll tell you, Lorraine,'' he promised her. ''Someday soon I'll tell you.''

She opened her mouth to say something when her

glance suddenly went past him and then her face was pale and taut with surprise and she sucked in her breath sharply. Harland released her and spun on a heel, his right hand starting to bring the .44 out of its holster, but then he saw who it was and Harland just froze, for the instant not knowing what to make of it.

The sorrel stood at the edge of the pines a short distance away and Mitch Antrim sat in the saddle. His head was bowed and he appeared to be very pre-occupied with the cigarette he was shaping. How long Antrim had been there Harland had no idea.

Finally, Antrim finished his cigarette and he popped the smoke in his mouth and sent the sorrel up to Harland and Lorraine. Antrim seemed to be pre-tending very hard that he had not noticed anything. However, he seemed a trifle pale about the mouth.

He fumbled in the pockets of his vest and then he said to Harland, "I seem to be out of matches."

Harland fished one out and handed it up. "Thanks, amigo," murmured Antrim. He looked at Lorraine. The shock had worn off and she had regained her composure. She had wiped her eyes and now she looked cool and even aloof.

"Hello, Lorraine," Antrim said. "I dropped by to see if you needed a hand. You're—you're all alone now and I thought maybe you needed help with the stock or something for a couple of days."

"I'm managing all right, Mitch. Thanks."

Antrim seemed rather uncomfortable. "I can lay off the bottle for two, three days if that's what you're worried about."

"Please don't say that, Mitch. I just don't need any help right now. Maybe later on, at round-up, but not now."

"Well, I thought I'd ask," said Antrim. He glanced

at Harland's saddle on the ground and then at Harland. "Were you riding, Harland? I'll wait for you and we'll ride together." He jingled some coins in a pocket and winked. "Maybe we can even stop in somewhere for a couple of snorts. What say, amigo?"

Harland roped his bay and saddled it. He did not look at Lorraine or say goodbye as he started off. He could feel her eyes following him and he wanted to turn and wave to her or just get one last look of her but he would not yield to the desire.

As they rode into the pines, Antrim sent his sorrel alongside the bay. For a while Antrim was silent. Then he said, "She's quite a girl, Harland."

"I didn't know you knew her."

"I've known her all my life. For a while I thought I was going to marry her but then she married Jim Lancaster. That was a long time ago, Harland."

They rode in silence for a long while after that.

Chapter Nine

Harland sat in the shade, across the street from the Ace of Diamonds, waiting for Jordan to come out. Jordan had ridden into town two hours before and gone directly to the saloon.

Harland was prepared to wait all day if necessary. Jordan was the logical next step in whatever vague plan Harland had to follow.

Finally Jordan appeared and mounted the palomino. Harland trotted to Beeson's Stable. He saddled his bay hurriedly and then spurred out of town, selecting a route that would take him around Jordan without being seen by the man. Harland rode hard. He swung far out from the trail to Bridlebit and then drove the bay hard for an hour parallel to the trail before angling back. He figured that now he was well ahead of Jordan, between him and Bridlebit.

Harland stopped the bay where the trail made an

abrupt drop down a small hill. At the foot of the hill grew a large cottonwood and some brush, and here Harland waited.

When Jordan appeared, he had the palomino moving at a lazy trot. Jordan was hunched over in the saddle, his hands folded over the horn, his head bowed as if he were dozing in the kak. Harland's bay whinnied and the palomino answered, and that alerted Jordan. His head flung up and he reined in the palomino hard so that the animal reared.

Harland was slouched over in the saddle. His grey eyes were narrowed slightly as they regarded Jordan. Harland said nothing.

Little beads of sweat broke out on Jordan's forehead. "Oh, it's you, Harland," he said.

"That's right," said Harland. "I was waiting for you, Jordan."

"Waiting for me?" Jordan repeated mechanically. "Why would you be doing that?"

Harland beckoned with his head. "Let's ride over to that bunch of aspens on that hill yonder and I'll tell you."

Jordan glanced apprehensively in the direction Harland had indicated. Jordan's fingers were nervously twisting the lines. "I've got to get to Bridlebit, Harland," he mumbled. "I'm in a hurry."

"This won't take long," said Harland. "If you cooperate, it won't take but a minute. Let's get going, Jordan."

"No," said Jordan. He had summoned up a bit of courage and the ordeal it was showed in the stark and pale cast of his face.

"No?" repeated Harland. He straightened in the saddle and his eyes stabbed at Jordan's waist where a holstered six-shooter hung. "I see you're packing an iron today," Harland said quietly.

"I'm no gunslinger," Jordan said hastily. He began to sweat copiously. "I'm no good with an iron, Harland. I've never used one in a fight. I've never looked for trouble, Harland."

"Then ride over to those aspens and you won't find trouble."

When Jordan hesitated, Harland dropped his voice to a growl and said, "Don't make me pull a gun on you, bucko!"

"All right," said Jordan, the tip of his tongue flicking at his lips. "But I can't stay more than a minute. They're waiting for me at Bridlebit. . . ."

Harland made Jordan lead the way. The grove of aspens stood a good two hundred yards from the trail. They rode into the trees unobserved by anyone. When they came to a small open spot Harland signalled Jordan to halt.

Harland dismounted. "You'd better get off your horse, too," he told Jordan.

Jordan stepped to the ground. He kept darting querying glances at Harland. "I'm expected at Bridlebit," he said again. "They're waiting for me there."

"Let them wait," said Harland. He began to build a smoke.

"If I'm not there when I'm supposed to be, they'll come looking for me," said Jordan. He sounded triumphant and pleased at what he had thought up.

"If they do," Harland said dryly, "they'll probably ride on to Edenville first and look in the Ace of Diamonds. By the time they get back here we should have our little chat over with." He finished the cigarette and extended it to Jordan. "Have a smoke, Jordan. It'll quieten your nerves."

"My nerves are all right," said Jordan, but he accepted the cigarette. His fingers shook as he placed it in his mouth. Harland struck a match and lighted Jordan's smoke for him.

Then Harland began to roll another cigarette for himself. While he worked, he said, "You can make it quick and easy for both of us, Jordan. I want to know who told you to tell me that you had hired Lancaster killed."

"No—no one told me to tell you," he stammered. "I—I—I told you on my own."

"You've never done anything on your own," Harland said cruelly, and Jordan flushed. Harland had completed his smoke and he popped it into his mouth. He struck a match on the seat of his Levi's and lighted the cigarette. "Who was it, Jordan?"

"I—I just told you. It was me."

"Was it Ace Lowrie?"

"Ace Low-Lowrie?" Jordan stuttered. He put the smoke back in his mouth and took two swift drags. "You must be crazy, Harland. It was like I told you. Lancaster was running off my stock and I couldn't stop him any other way so I decided to have someone kill him."

"You can stop giving me that," Harland said coldly, "because I don't believe a word of it." His eyes narrowed and glittered uglily as he stared at Jordan. "You better tell me, Jordan," he said quietly.

"But—but it's true," Jordan insisted. His voice was high and it cracked now and then. "You—you must know the kind of hombre Lancaster was. He was a hardcase, a—a troublemaker. You've probably heard the talk that he held up that Border Pacific pay car. There's a railroad detective around looking for Lancaster." His eyes suddenly widened. "Is that why

99

you're here? Are you after Lancaster for something? Are you with the law?''

Harland could not help a grim smile. "I'm no lawman." Then the smile died. "What does Lowrie have to do with this?''

"I don't know where you got this crazy idea about Ace Lowrie, Harland. Sure, I know Ace. I stop in his place all the time, but I stop in other saloons in Edenville, too. That doesn't mean a thing. Hell, Ace sells liquor, and when I feel like a drink I stop in his place or go somewhere else. What's wrong with that?''

"That day you had me come out to Bridlebit, why was Dude Prentiss there?''

"It's like I told you. Dude's a friend of mine. He always comes out to Bridlebit. And I—I was scared of you, Harland. That's why I wanted Dude around.''

"Doesn't Prentiss work for Lowrie?''

"Ye-yes.''

"Was it Lowrie who put you up to telling me you had Lancaster killed? Was it Lowrie who sent Prentiss out to Bridlebit to protect you in case I got tough— and to make sure you said what you were supposed to say?''

"No!'' Jordan almost screamed the word. He held his hands up appealingly. "Won't you believe me, Harland? I've told you how it was. Lancaster was a train robber. Couldn't he have been a rustler, too?''

"If he had that hundred thousand from the pay car stick-up, why would he fool around with rustling a few head of cattle?''

"That—that was before he held up the train. He probably wasn't doing good enough at rustling, so he decided to stick up a train.''

"You know, Jordan,'' Harland said softly, "you haven't told me a thing.''

Jordan spread his hands in helplessness. "I—I—I've told you all I know," he stammered, staring fearfully at Harland's face.

Harland's lips were a thin white line. Anger showed in the bulging of the muscles along his jaw and in the glare in his eyes. His voice was low and thick from the imposition of a severe control.

"Listen, Jordan," he growled, "I didn't ask you to come into this. You were the one who sent for me. I didn't even know you were alive until you had me come out to Bridlebit. You bought into this game and you're in it to stay. There's no cashing in chips in this game. You're in it until the last hand's been played." He drew a deep breath while he struggled to keep the rage from bursting out of him. "For the last time, Jordan. Are you going to tell me who put you up to claiming you had Lancaster killed?"

"No—no one put me up. I did it myself."

"Drop your gunbelt, Jordan," said Harland.

Jordan's eyes flared with terror. "What are you going to do?"

"If you'd rather use your gun, it's all right with me."

"No, no," Jordan exclaimed hastily. "I'm no gunslinger. I'm no good on the draw and shoot." He unbuckled his shell belt and allowed it to fall to the ground. "What are you going to do, Harland?" His voice was scarcely above a whisper.

Harland removed his own belt and gun and hung them from his saddlehorn. Then he turned and looked at Jordan. "I'd say I'm spotting you twenty or more pounds, Jordan. That should be fair enough, shouldn't it?" He advanced on Jordan.

"I don't want to fight," said Jordan, licking his lips.

"Neither do I," said Harland. "Tell me what I want to know and there won't be any need to fight."

Jordan said nothing. He began backing up and Harland cursed in a sudden fit of unbearable rage and rushed at him. He swung a looping right at Jordan's head, but the man stopped abruptly and swayed aside and lashed out swiftly with a blow that caught Harland high on the head. The force of it started Harland's ears ringing and he fell back, more in astonishment that Jordan had struck back than in pain.

Jordan seemed to gather courage from this. He bore ahead, swinging, and he landed two more blows, one against Harland's chest, the other on Harland's shoulder. Harland stopped going back. He planted his feet and hooked a left with all his strength at the paunch that was beginning to show in Jordan's middle. The wind ripped out of Jordan and he gasped retchingly and started to go back.

Harland drove in, full of a raging fury now. He swung at Jordan's head but the man ducked and threw up an arm, deflecting Harland's blow. Again Harland hooked at Jordan's paunch and when the fellow gasped and dropped his arms to cover his stomach, Harland caught him on the cheek. The blow sent Jordan sprawling.

He made no move to get up. He lay where he had fallen and he buried his face in his arms and began to sob. "Go ahead and kill me," he cried. "I've told you all I know."

Quivering with rage, Harland stood over him. "Get up, Jordan," he snarled. "I've just begun. Get up on your feet like a man."

Jordan did not stir. He kept his face concealed in the hollow of his arms. His voice came, muffled and thick with shame. "I'm no fighting man. I'm licked.

102

I've told you all I can tell you. If that isn't enough, then you can kill me, Harland. I don't care what you do to me. I won't fight back. Go ahead and kill me.''

Harland could have wept with frustration. The whole thing gagged him, he had no stomach for it any more. He was hard and tough and relentless, but he could not bring himself to fight a man who would not fight back. What he needed was a temperament like Worthington's, Harland thought bitterly. Worthington would make Jordan talk. He'd have Jordan spilling his guts in no time at all, but those were doings for a man like Worthington, Harland thought, not for him.

Harland spun on his heel and went over to his bay. He strapped on his gun and swung up into the saddle. At the creak of saddle leather, Jordan stopped sobbing and lifted his face from his arms. He stared at Harland as if he could not believe what he saw.

Harland's lips were pale with rage at his own softness and ineptitude. He scorned to look at Jordan. Harland jabbed the bay with his spurs and sent it at a fast run out of the aspens.

The next morning, back in Edenville, Harland was walking towards Lowrie's saloon when he heard the rush of pounding hooves behind him. He was walking in the street, and now he veered over to the side to give whoever it was in such a hurry plenty of room. At the last instant it dawned on Harland that the horse behind him had veered with him.

He whirled, startled, and the palomino was upon him. The horse cut between Harland and the buildings and the fore shoulders of the palomino struck him and sent him hurtling out into the street. He tried to retain his balance, but his legs tangled and he went down

103

in a heap. He jumped to his feet as fast as he could, but by this time the palomino had been turned and was bearing down on him again.

Shock and consternation gave way to a boiling rage in Harland. He reached for his gun and started to bring it up when he saw who it was on the palomino.

The rider was Glennis Jordan.

The palomino kicked up dust and grit with the speed of its running. This time, however, the horse was not aimed at Harland. It sped past him and Glennis Jordan leaned out from the saddle and brought her arm down. The quirt in her hand slashed at Harland's face. He saw it coming and he threw up his arms, but he was too late. The lash curled about his cheek and stung and cut and a bright sear of pain blinded his eyes. Then the palomino was past him.

He stood there, gun in hand, and watched the girl spin the horse around and start another run at him. Her face was contorted with fury; she was all rage and hate. This time she reined the palomino down as the horse reached Harland. She sent the animal crowding up against Harland and her quirt began to flail.

Her voice was thick with wrath. "I warned you, Harland," she snarled at him. "I told you to leave my brother alone. Maybe this will pound some sense into your thick skull."

The gun was no good in Harland's hand. He could not use it on her. The palomino kept crowding him; the girl skilfully kept one fore shoulder of the horse smashing up against Harland, forcing him off balance, while the quirt in her hand slashed blow after blow on his head and face and shoulders.

He could not flee from the whip. So he did the only thing left to him. Clenching his teeth, he took another lash in the face, but before the girl could pull the quirt away and raise it, Harland had grasped the whip. The quirt was looped about the girl's wrist. Harland stepped back and gave a yank to the quirt the same instant that the palomino lunged away from him.

A shrill scream emitted from the girl. She came tumbling out of the saddle as the palomino, frightened, raced away down the street. A fierce resentment filled Harland. He had never felt so helpless, so frustrated as those instants she had been whipping him.

He grabbed her as she bounded to her feet. For a moment he glared down at her hate-twisted face, an unreasoning rage pounding at his brain. He wanted to get back at her. He could not strike her, he could not use a gun on her for she was a woman. But he wanted to humiliate her.

He became conscious of many people watching and in that instant he knew what he was going to do. Roughly he jerked her against himself. She fought him. She twisted and pulled, she kicked at his shins, she averted her face time and again, but he would not be denied. His mouth finally found hers and he held her like that for half a minute. He could feel her whole body trembling with helplessness and rage. Her lips were cold and writhed away from his in repugnance. But she could not break away from him until he released her.

Her face was scarlet and she stood there, confused by rage and hate and uncertainty. Her breasts heaved with the wrath that boiled in her. She started to raise her right arm again when Harland said in a low, determined tone:

"Do you remember what I told you once? I'll use that quirt on you right where you sit down. You touch me just once more with it, Miss Jordan, and I'll do what I promised—right in front of all these people.''

She saw that he meant it. Slowly, her arm lowered
and she bit her lip in indecision and bewilderment.
But the hate flared as bright as ever in her eyes.

"Next time, Harland," she told him, "I won't use
a whip. I'll use a gun!"

"Thanks for warning me."

He watched as she walked off with short, stiff,
wrathful strides. In his ears sounded the slow, mea-
sured pounding of his heart.

Chapter Ten

Mist still lingered in the low spots when Harland rode out of Edenville early the next morning. In his heart there was a sense of misgiving, of wrongness, and he tried to shrug it from himself, but it would not go.

He cut across the valley towards that spur of the Stalwarts where Lancaster's ranch lay. He had thought that if he could see Lorraine again it might solve something; it might ease and soothe the uncertainty and the feeling of evil. But as the bay travelled ever higher on the slopes, instead of eagerness in himself Harland encountered a growing reluctance. The moment came that he shunned the thought of seeing Lorraine Lancaster today.

He reined in the bay, not certain any more what he wanted to do. He glanced about him with vexation. He was in the crevice between two slopes. The ground rose gently on either side of him. As usual, he had stuck to the more open land. It was the old innate caution.

Both slopes rose to great heights. High above on either side of him the dark green line of the timber stretched. Below this there were only a few straggling pines and junipers and the occasional rough, harsh out-thrust of a stone escarpment. The buffalo grass was a foot high here, the tops of it waving gently in a small breeze.

Then the rider appeared.

He came out of the timber far above Harland and halted his horse there while he stared down the long length of the slope at Harland. Something that he could not define warned Harland. His throat went dry. He shifted around in the kak and glanced up the opposite slope and up there, too, just below the timber, was another horseman.

There was something ominous and malignant in the way the two sat their horses so still and stared down at him with deliberate concentration. Little cold feet travelled up and down Harland's spine.

He could make a run for it, he thought, but there was one on either side of him, and they could run with him, angling down the slopes at him at the same time, and Harland dismissed running from his mind. He could only sit and wait. The deal belonged to them; they were the ones who would call the game.

He kept glancing first at one and then at the other. His fingers itched for the Winchester in the saddle boot beneath his thigh, but he did not want to make the first hostile move. He would leave that up to them for perhaps violence was not their desire. But this was a faint, futile hope in Harland. From the way they regarded him, from the way they had suddenly appeared one on either side, he knew that peace was not their intention.

Still neither rider moved. They just sat in their saddles, way up there on the slopes, far enough beyond recognition, looking down at him, studying him as if they were still undecided as to what course to take. Harland began to sweat a little. He hoped they would commit themselves one way or another before too long. It was the waiting that grated at his nerves, not the fear of the consequences.

Finally, they moved. There was no signal. First the one on Harland's left started his horse, and when Harland swiftly looked up the opposite slope he saw that rider, too, was in motion. They were in no hurry. Their horses came down the slopes at a walk.

Harland looked about for cover. There was only the foot-high grass and an occasional stone, nothing promising or effective. Harland decided he had waited enough. He drew out his Winchester.

The two riders saw this and they, too, took their rifles in their hands. But they made no move to fire. They kept coming down the slopes with their horses at a walk. Harland held his Winchester ready, watching first one then the other through slitted eyes.

They came on and took shape and finally Harland recognised them—Ike Gibson and Bronco Curtis. At this point they reined in their mounts.

Gibson rose up in his stirrups and shouted at the top of his voice, but still the words were faint and barely audible to Harland.

"We've got you, Harland," Gibson shouted. "Throw down your gun and raise your hands."

Harland's heart was beating with a slow, leaden excitement. Now that he knew who they were, he could guess what they wanted, and he could use this knowledge to guide his actions. He said nothing. He sat there in his kak as if on pinpoints, ready to hit the ground at the first alarming move by either of the two.

"Did you hear me, Harland?" Gibson shouted, raising his rifle menacingly.

They were two to his one, Harland thought, they had him in a crossfire between them, but still the advantage lay with him. He was sure of that. He knew what they wanted from him and this, he was positive, gave him the edge over them.

He snapped off a shot up at Gibson, and before the startled men could retaliate, Harland was going out of the saddle. He hit the grass as one bullet, then another, whined over him. He had kicked the bay with a spur just before quitting his seat and the horse went racing off, out of the line of fire.

Harland rolled over and over on the ground until he dropped into a small depression. He lay there, hugging the earth, while Gibson and Curtis scorched the air over him with screaming slugs. Harland waited patiently, flinching now and then as a slug came over too close. Finally, Gibson and Curtis became tired of wasting shells. The last echoes of the gunshots went rolling up the mountain and silence settled in.

After a while, Gibson started to shout again. He sounded as if he had worked down a little closer. "You might as well give up, Harland. We've got you good. Give up peaceful-like if you don't want to die with a hot slug in your belly!"

Harland did not answer. He smiled grimly, thinking that he was gambling his life on what he supposed was in their minds. He could not, however, be sure of it. He could be very wrong—in which instance he'd die. He decided now was the time to find out.

His heart was hammering as he crawled carefully

out of the hollow, keeping down low so as to use the bunches of grass to shield his intent and purpose. Gibson was on the slope to Harland's left, Curtis on the slope to the right. Harland chose Curtis as his quarry since he was convinced Curtis was not as bright as Gibson.

Harland moved perhaps ten feet before they spotted him. A roar of rage emanated from Gibson and then both their rifles opened up. A boulder loomed several feet ahead of Harland and he scrambled as hastily as he could for its shelter. Even so, one slug raked his back, and he could feel the sting of it and the blood started to run as he reached the boulder. However, he did not think it was anything serious.

He lay flat on his belly behind the boulder while bullets shrieked and whined as they ricocheted off the stone. Again he waited patiently until Gibson and Curtis tired of wasting cartridges. Then while they either rested or reloaded, Harland rose up on his elbows for a quick look around.

The two had both dismounted. On the far slope, Gibson lay flat atop a rock escarpment. On this slope, Curtis had taken up a post behind the meagre and dubious cover of a stunted pine. Harland could feel his heart hammering against his ribs.

He took a deep breath and then he shouted, "I'm coming for you, Bronco!"

Curtis sent a mocking laugh down the slope. "Come right up, Harland. I'm waiting for you."

"I'll come in a minute, Bronco, but I want to tell you something first," shouted Harland. Sweat trickled down into his eyes. The corners of his mouth were stiff with tension. "You don't dare kill me, Bronco. You've got to wing me. I'm no good to you dead. How will you find out where the money is if I'm dead? Lancaster's gone. He can't tell you any more. I'm the only living man who knows where that money is buried. You get me, Bronco? You've got to be sure you wing me. You can't take a chance on killing me!''

He paused to listen to what Curtis had to say in return. But Curtis was silent.

He did not like the idea of putting his back to Gibson, but Gibson was pretty far away and then, if Harland had surmised correctly, Gibson, too, would have to exercise care with his shooting. I can only die once, Harland thought, and he bolted to his feet and went charging up the slope.

He had the Winchester at his hip and he began spraying bullets at the pine behind which Curtis crouched. Curtis opened up the instant that Harland showed. Gibson, also, began to fire, but every step Harland took carried him farther from Gibson.

Curtis's first shot nicked the edge of Harland's Levi's, but that was the closest Curtis came. He was obviously rattled. Harland charged with a weaving run, swaying from side to side, ducking his shoulders. When Curtis saw that he was not placing his slugs where he wanted them, he edged out farther from behind the pine for a better aim. It was then that Harland got him.

The .44 slug took Curtis in the neck. He came upright as though prodded by a red-hot iron. His arms flung up and he clawed at the sky. His head hurled back, revealing the gaping hole in his neck, and then the blood began to gush. His fingers rose and clawed at his throat and his mouth made horrible gasping, racking sounds. He took two steps forward, the clawing motions of his hands slowing. Then he pressed the palms of both hands against the wound as if that would stop the flow of blood. The next instant his knees buckled and threw him forward on his face. He was dead.

Harland spun, the Winchester at his shoulder, his eyes searching the opposite slope. Gibson, however, had had enough. He was legging it as fast as he could for his mount. Harland tried two shots, but the range was too long for accuracy. Gibson mounted and sent his horse at a lunging run up the slope. He was soon gone into the timber, leaving Harland alone with the dead man.

Overhead, a vulture wheeled.

Harland left Bronco Curtis where he had fallen. If Ike Gibson cared, he could return for the body of his partner. Or, if he preferred, he could leave the disposal of Curtis's corpse to the natural inclinations of the vultures, two of which now floated overhead. Harland did not much care.

The bay had not fled far, and Harland walked up to it and mounted. He sent the horse back in the direction from which he had come. The bay entered a small mountain meadow and all at once a rider appeared out of the trees across the open stretch of ground. Harland's .44 was clear of its holster before recognition came to him. The rider was Mitch Antrim.

When Antrim spotted Harland, the redhead turned his sorrel in that direction. Harland put up his six-shooter. He reined in the bay and waited for Antrim to come up. Antrim's face was bland, but there seemed to be a keen interest in his eyes as he studied Harland.

Antrim took out tobacco and papers and began to fashion a smoke. His head was bowed and he seemed to be devoting all his attention to the cigarette. ''I

heard some shooting a while back,'' he said. He rolled
the paper into a tight cylinder and then he raised it to
his lips and licked the paper. As he did this, his eyes
speared Harland. ''Was it you, amigo?''

Harland smiled grimly. ''Ike Gibson and Bronco
Curtis jumped me. I got Curtis and when that happened Gibson lost his appetite and high-tailed it.''

''I always figured Bronco would end up like this,''
said Antrim. He was searching the pockets of his vest.
''I know I've got a match somewhere,'' he muttered.

Harland fished one out and handed it over.
''Thanks, amigo,'' said Antrim. He laid a warm, genuine smile on Harland. That smile remained on Antrim's face while he savoured the first two puffs of
his smoke. Then the smile faded and Antrim's face
turned almost hard and he leaned forward slightly in
his saddle.

''Listen, Harland,'' he said earnestly, ''I'm your
friend. I'm telling you this for your own good.
There's nothing here in the Stalwarts but trouble for
you, Harland. Take my advice, amigo, and ride on.''

''How do you know there will be trouble for me?''
asked Harland.

Antrim lifted his brows as if the question were very
stupid. ''What was that you just went through, amigo?
The Fourth of July?''

The bullet graze on Harland's back twinged a little.
An overwhelming irritation swept over him. ''I can
take care of myself,'' he muttered grimly.

''No doubt you can,'' agreed Antrim. He was staring at the tip of his smoke as if he were considering
very carefully what he was going to say. ''You don't
know what you're getting into, Harland,'' Antrim said
after a short pause. ''You're digging into something
that's ended. Why don't you leave it like that?''

"What's ended, Mitch?" asked Harland.

Antrim shrugged. "Lancaster's dead, isn't he?"

"Is he?"

Antrim smiled faintly. "All right, you don't have to tell me. But if Lancaster's dead, then you killed him. Can't you leave it like that?" His glance lifted now to Harland's face. There was an appeal in Antrim's eyes. "Can't you, amigo?"

Harland could feel his mind working at something. He could feel the pieces in his grasp but he could not determine how to fit them together. All that resulted in him was a sense of utter futility.

"Where do you fit into this, Mitch?" asked Harland.

"I don't fit in anywhere."

"Would you have any idea who wanted Lancaster dead?"

"No."

"Why are you asking me to ride on, then?"

Antrim spread his hands in exasperation. "I like you, amigo," he said again. "I'd hate to see you get killed."

"Who would want to kill me?"

"Gibson tried, didn't he? He'll try again."

"I can handle Gibson."

"Gibson might not be the only one."

"Who else would there be?" persisted Harland.

Antrim spread his hands again. "You know as much about that as I do, amigo."

"What do you know about Lancaster, Mitch?"

Pain showed deep and faintly luminous in Antrim's eyes. "I knew Jim Lancaster all my life. We were never pals but we were never enemies, either, not even when he married Lorraine." That hurt became brighter in his glance. "Can't you see, amigo? It's for her. Lancaster's dead and she should start forgetting about him. Isn't that right? But you keep digging it up and it keeps coming back to her and she just gets hurt over and over. If you rode away, the whole thing would die and she'd forget and that would be good for everybody. Don't you see, Harland?" He was pleading.

A form of understanding came to Harland. He could appreciate how Antrim must feel, for Antrim's love for Lorraine Lancaster had been as hopeless and bitter as Harland's was right now.

"I'm sorry, Mitch," Harland murmured.

"But why?" Antrim cried. "You killed Lancaster and now you want to avenge him. It doesn't make sense."

"I'm sorry," Harland said again.

Antrim settled back in his kak and took a long, solemn look at Harland's face. He studied the stubborn cast of Harland's jaw, the cold, unrelenting purpose in Harland's eyes. Antrim saw how it was and how it would be and he sighed in defeat.

"All right, amigo," he said. "I tried." He kneed the sorrel over beside the bay and clapped Harland on the back. There was a crooked grin on Antrim's mouth. "Life's too short to sit around and argue. Let's go wet our whistles. What do you say, amigo?"

Chapter Eleven

The sun dropped behind the Stalwarts and the long shadows crept softly across the valley and the air thickened and grew chill. Harland kept hearing Mitch Antrim's argument over and over. Ride on, Harland, ride on, Antrim's voice seemed to be whispering in his ear. You're doing no good in the Stalwarts. You're just bringing trouble and pain. You keep opening the grave and that's no good. Ride on, amigo. . . .

Harland was so caught up in his troubled reflections that he was not aware of the rider coming towards him until he was only twenty feet away. A horse whinnied softly and the bay answered, and that roused Harland. His head flung up and his first instinct was to snatch at his .44, but then he saw who it was and he took his hand away.

The rider on the palomino was Glennis Jordan.

She pulled up the palomino and motioned Harland

to stop. Night was starting to close in and in the thickening gloom her face looked wan and even distraught. But perhaps that was due to the twilight, Harland thought, and his own dark mood.

She appeared as if she were trying to talk but could not find any words. Finally she said, "I'd like to apologise to you, Harland."

She was close enough now so that her knee touched his leg. She leaned slightly towards him, her face turned up to him. "Aren't you going to help, Harland?" she said. "This isn't easy for me. I'm not used to humbling myself. Won't you say something? Won't you tell me I'm forgiven?"

For an instant, Harland was aware only of her nearness. He could feel his blood begin to pound, his throat filled with a cloying ache as he realised for the first time what she could really do to him. Then she edged still closer, and it was this small movement that told Harland something was wrong.

She was to the right of him and she was leaning so close to him that she almost touched. He sensed rather than saw her reach for his gun. Harland grabbed for her hand, but she had already gripped the butt of the .44 and she jerked it out of its holster and started to pull away from him with her mouth twisting into a grimace of hate.

Harland grunted with surprise and anger and he struck out with the flat of his hand, hitting her wrist and knocking the gun upwards as it went off. The slug missed his hat and went screaming off at the sky. She swung her arm around and away as he sought to grasp it. Then she started to bring the .44 down to bear on him again.

He pulled hard on the lines and rammed the bay up against the palomino. The jolt almost unseated

Glennis Jordan. She cried out in alarm and fright and the .44 exploded, but the barrel had wavered way out of line and this slug, too, shrieked off harmlessly into the night. Before she could recover her balance, Harland had her wrist firmly in his grip.

"Let me go," she cried, voice thick with fury. "I'm going to kill you!"

He started to twist her arm to force her to drop the gun, but she brought her left arm around in a round-house swing that connected with the side of his face. The unexpectedness of it caused him to relax his hold and the girl jerked her hand free.

He grabbed for her instantly. When she saw that she could not aim the .44, she raised the gun high, swung the palomino hard against the bay, and started to bring the long barrel of the .44 down towards Harland's head. He reached and ducked and swayed aside. Even so, the barrel smashed down on his shoulder, but before the girl could lift the gun for another try, he had her wrist again.

She started another swing with her free hand but Harland raised his right arm and blocked it. He caught this arm, too, and held it tightly. Now that she was imprisoned, the girl's rage seemed to double. She rose in her stirrups and jerked and tugged, and once she ducked her head and tried to sink her teeth into his hand.

She would not quit struggling. "I am going to kill you," she kept muttering over and over. "I am going to kill you." Her face was grey with hate and vicious purpose.

"Not if I can help it," Harland growled. He was beginning to sweat from his efforts to subdue her.

"I am going to kill you."

"Why? Will you tell me that?"

"I'm going to kill you like you killed my brother!"

"I don't know what you're talking about!"

"You killed him and I'm killing you!"

"Will you calm down and take it easy? I tell you I don't know anything about your brother."

"You killed him! You killed him!"

"How do you know I killed him?"

"You're a killer, aren't you? Killing people is your business, isn't it?"

Harland gave a sudden powerful twist to the girl's arm and she screamed in pain and the .44 hung lax in her hand. He snatched the gun away.

The fight went abruptly out of the girl. Her struggles ceased and she sat there in her saddle with her head bowed while gasping sobs began to rack her.

Harland released her wrist and then he settled back in his kak while he stared at her. She made no move to flee. She sat hunched over on the palomino, and now she placed her hands over her face and the harshness went out of her sobs and she began to weep softly.

When she finally looked at him, she was dry-eyed and the old hate was strong in her face once more.

"There'll come a day, Harland," she said, her voice thick with animosity. "This thing is far from ended between you and me."

She would have gone then, but Harland reached out and caught the palomino's bridle. His voice was harsh and strained from the effort he was putting out to contain himself. "There are a few things I'd like to know from you. Since someday you're going to kill me," he said dryly, "I feel I'm entitled to know them." His tone became gentle. "I'm sorry about your brother. I can guess what he meant to you. Believe me, I'm telling the truth when I say I didn't know he was dead until you told me." He took a deep breath. "However, if you want to keep on holding me responsible for his death, I can't stop you. But tell me this. What makes you so sure I was the one who killed him?"

"You had trouble with him, didn't you? You beat him up, didn't you?"

Harland leaned back in the saddle and stared at her thoughtfully. "That's hardly enough proof," he said quietly.

She made an angry, exasperated gesture. "I know it. I rode into Edenville to see if I could get a warrant for your arrest, but they told me it was no use, that you could get out of it. Oh, you're a smart one, Harland," she said bitterly. "You know how to cover your trail, don't you?"

"Will you listen to me?" he shouted at her so wrathfully that she flinched. "Who are you to set yourself up as a judge of anybody? What do you really know about me? All that you know is what you've heard and what you've heard has all been dirty, stinking rumours and gossip. How do you know I'm a dirty, sneaking killer? Have you ever seen me kill?"

His whole body was trembling with rage. All the frustration and helplessness and hurt he had suffered over the years for his predicament vented out of him with his words.

"Everyone pretends to know why I've come to the Stalwarts," he cried. "I've told no one but that makes no difference. Everybody is sure they know what goes on in my mind. Well, for the first time I'm going to tell someone what I'm doing here. I'm telling you, Miss Jordan.

"You're right about me in one respect. I am a

121

killer! I've killed in the past and maybe it's in the cards for me to kill in the future, if somebody doesn't get me first. But every man that I've killed I've dropped from the front. I've given every man I've ever faced an even break. I've gambled my life against his. And that's why I'm here in the Stalwarts.''

He was perspiring freely now, whether from anger or bitterness or the intensity of his emotions Harland did not know. ''I am not trying to hold myself up as an honest, respectable man,'' he went on. ''I am not trying to excuse the fact that I hired out to kill a man. The man I was paid to kill was Jim Lancaster.'' Harland could feel the pound of the pulse in his temple. The words poured out of him like a torrent which he could not halt. ''If I was the dirty, sneaking killer you say I am, I would have taken the easy way. I would have dropped Lancaster from the back and then I'd have ridden away and that would have been the end of that. Instead, I faced Lancaster. I gambled my speed with a gun against his—and I lost!''

She seemed to be cringing in the saddle, transfixed with awe by the force and fury of his speech. He plunged on, the words coming out of him without thinking, just rushing out of his heart, carrying with them the anguish and rancour he had endured for so long.

''Did you hear me? I gambled my life against Lancaster's and I lost—yet I'm still alive, and that's why I'm here in the Stalwarts. Lancaster was faster with a gun than I was. He had me beat but he didn't fire. It all happened so fast I had already pulled my trigger before I realised he was not going to shoot. So Lancaster's dead now. He's dead in my place. You understand? I'm alive only because Lancaster wanted to die, and I want to know why he wanted to die and who wanted him dead.

"Maybe Lancaster wasn't much of a man. From what I've learned of him I don't think he ever amounted to much. But I owe him something, I owe him my life. Maybe it's crazy, twisted thinking, but that's the way I feel about it. I took money to kill Lancaster but I know that I will never take money to kill a man again. I owe that, too, to Jim Lancaster. Maybe he was no good. Maybe he was a train robber and a rustler, but I'm going to square for him."

He rose in the stirrups and leaned towards the girl and tapped her on the chest with a finger. She sat in the saddle as if mesmerised, hardly breathing as she listened to him.

"And in squaring for Lancaster, I'll be squaring for your brother, too. Somehow, he got mixed up in it. Why that was I don't know. But whoever it was that killed your brother did it because your brother could have told me what I want to know. There you have it, Miss Jordan," he said bitterly, settling back in his saddle. "It's all so crazy and mixed up I don't expect you to believe any of it, and I don't care. You say you're going to kill me some day. You're perfectly welcome to go ahead and try it. Life isn't so sweet to me that I'm afraid to lose it."

With that Harland touched the bay with the spurs and sent it off at a hard run.

When he reached Edenville, Harland was in an ugly mood. He had been through a lot this day. He had been shot at. He had killed a man. He had had another run-in with Glennis Jordan. The sum of them left him irascible and tired, but he suspected that if he went to bed he would find no rest. It was the

123

thought of lying awake another night with his mind haunted by needling recollections and self-recriminations that angered him more than anything else.

He was also exasperated by his inability to get anywhere with this job which he had taken upon himself. There was that tantalising feeling in him that he already knew as much as he needed to know to solve the riddle of Lancaster's death. The key to it, he was sure, lurked just beyond the edges of his comprehension, but, try as he might, he could not break through that invisible, impenetrable barrier to obtain the knowledge he strove for. It left him feeling weak and helpless and infuriated.

Harland put up the bay at Beeson's and then he struck out across the night-shrouded town for the Lamar House. The sky was clouded now, shutting out the stars, and there was the rumble of thunder from high up in the Stalwarts. The heavens were rifted now and then by the swift, sharp shimmering of lightning.

The man stepped out of Masterson's Mercantile and halted, framed in the yellow lamplight spilling out of Masterson's open doorway, while he lit his pipe. On the street below, Harland stopped abruptly, an instant, vicious anger tearing at his mind. The man in front of Masterson's was Cal Worthington.

At first, Worthington did not notice Harland. His pipe going, Worthington stepped down into the street and took two steps, and it was only then he became aware of Harland, standing there immobile.

Worthington pulled up with a start that evoked a faint jingle from his spurs. The light was at his back and thus his face was shaded, but Harland could still make out the pale ovals that were the lenses of Worthington's spectacles. Once Worthington had stopped, he moved no more.

After a minute, Harland started ahead slowly. Each step he took seemed to add to his wrath. The humiliation, the pain, the despair he had felt that time, all came roaring back to Harland in a veritable whirlwind of remembrance. Even the muscles of his thighs trembled from the rage that diffused through him.

Worthington stood there as if transmuted into stone. Harland halted in front of him. He planted his feet firmly and then, his voice quivering with fury, he said, "I'm not going to tie you to a post, Worthington. I'm not going to stake you out in the sun. I'm not going to keep you without food or water. I'm going to be quick with you, Worthington. I'm doing it like this."

He raised his left hand and brought the back of it crashing against the side of Worthington's face. The force of the blow turned the man's head half around and knocked his spectacles awry and sent the pipe flying out of his mouth. Worthington fell back half a step, involuntarily, and there he stopped. He made not a sound. He lifted his right hand and adjusted his glasses. Then he stood there, silently staring at Harland.

"I know I'm a gunfighter," Harland growled when Worthington made no effort to speak. "I know I'm pretty good with an iron. But I didn't ask to get mixed up with you. You started it, Worthington. Now I'm carrying it to a finish. You can draw any time you're ready."

Worthington shook his head slowly, with a quiet deliberation. "I'm not drawing against you, Harland," he said.

Harland's eyes were aching slits of hate and venomous purpose. Wrath and indignation kept bouncing against his brain. "You can pull first," he told Worthington. "I'll give you that much of a break."

Again Worthington shook his head. "The railroad doesn't pay me to go around shooting it out with professional gunmen. My job is very different from that." He took a deep breath. "I'm giving you my apology, Harland. I was wrong about you. I made a mistake about you. I realise that words can't make up for what you—endured. I lost my head and I'm sorry and ashamed for what I did. I'm apologising and I'm willing to do anything else to try to make it up to you, but I'm not drawing against you."

"You'll draw all right," Harland snarled, "if I have to slap you all over Edenville."

"I'll never draw," said Worthington. With his left hand he loosed the buckle of his gunbelt and let his holstered six-shooter drop to the ground. "I'll never draw."

A sensation of defeat descended on Harland. He knew he was thwarted again. He raised his left hand to strike Worthington again, but realised it would do no good. Even in his humiliation Worthington was the victor. Harland could have wept at his sense of impotency.

Still, Harland could not bring himself to give the matter up without one tiny measure of satisfaction. He had brooded over it so much, he had known so much mortification that he had to pay it back one way or another.

He struck out suddenly, viciously, with his fist. He put all his weight and strength behind the blow. If Worthington saw it coming, he made no move to evade it. He took the full force of it on his jaw and he went stumbling back a couple of steps, and then his knees gave way and he collapsed to the ground.

Harland stared for half a minute at Worthington's limp, motionless form. Then he turned and strode away. Instead of elation, there was the taste of gall in his mouth.

Chapter Twelve

That morning, after breakfast, Harland passed through the lobby of the Lamar House and went outside. On the gallery, he paused and built a smoke. While lighting it, he spied someone crossing the street towards him. It was Dude Prentiss.

Harland took a deep drag on his smoke and then held it in his left hand while with narrowed eyes he watched Prentiss approaching. There was that studied insolence again in Prentiss's manner, and Harland felt a surge of brittle anger. He had rested surprisingly well the night before but he still felt faintly on edge.

Prentiss did not mount the floor of the gallery. He stayed down in the street and lifted his left boot and placed it down on the floor which was about a foot above the surface of the street. The breeze carried a strong whiff of cologne to Harland's nostrils.

"Ace wants to see you," said Prentiss.

"Does he?" murmured Harland.

Prentiss jerked a thumb over his shoulder. His eyes were bright with arrogance. "He's waiting for you at the Ace of Diamonds."

"Let him wait."

Prentiss flushed. His mouth twitched with anger. "You coming, Harland?" he snapped.

Harland dropped his cigarette and carefully ground it out. He felt mean and ugly inside and kept hoping Prentiss would start something. "Has it occurred to you that I might not want to see Lowrie?"

"You think you're high and mighty, don't you, Harland?"

"I do. You care to make anything of it, Prentiss?"

The coldness of Harland's tone made Prentiss pause. The insolence went out of his eyes. In its place there came a calculative wariness. "Ace didn't send me to pick a fight with you," he said after a while. "You'd better come and see him, Harland—if you know what's good for you."

"Who's going to make me come?" said Harland with a sneer. "You?"

Prentiss flushed again. The fingers of his right hand twitched. Harland saw and he tensed, ready to grab at his own .44, but fight was not Prentiss's intention. He raised his right hand and hooked his thumb in his belt buckle.

His voice was deceptively gentle. "You've been pretty lucky so far, Harland, but don't let it go to your head. You can be taken care of one way or another. Personally, I don't give a damn whether you go to see Ace. I only work for him. He sent me to tell you and I've told you. What you do now is entirely up to you." He paused while his eyes glared malevolently. "As for me," he went on softly, "I'll just wait and see what Ace decides. He's a poor man to cross, Harland. Remember that."

With that, Prentiss spun on his heel and walked away.

Harland built himself another cigarette and after he had smoked it down, he finally left the Lamar House. He made his way leisurely across town to the Ace of Diamonds. There was a burning compulsion in him to find out what Lowrie wanted, but Harland also wanted to conceal this anxiousness, and so he took his time before calling on Ace Lowrie.

There was a feeling in him this morning that he was closer to the end of his job than he had anticipated. The killing of Will Jordan seemed to indicate this. Whoever it was behind the death of Lancaster might have feared that Jordan would eventually talk. So to silence Jordan, he was killed.

This idea of being close to the final solution but still not having any comprehension as to its complexion vexed Harland. He told himself it did no good if he became irritable and upset because of it. It was best if he just took it as it developed and did not try to rush it at all. He had been patient thus far, and perhaps with a little more patience he would finally see the end of it. The fact that Ace Lowrie had sent for him was proof that Harland was making progress. Harland could think of no other reason why Lowrie would want to see him.

At this hour of morning the Ace of Diamonds was devoid of customers. A swamper was cleaning up in the back and the lone bartender was wiping glasses since he had nothing else to do. The only other people in the saloon were Ace Lowrie and Dude Prentiss.

Lowrie and Prentiss stood at the bar with a bottle

between them. At the sound of Harland's spur jingle, Prentiss turned his head in that direction. When he saw who it was, Prentiss nudged Lowrie.

Lowrie turned with a slow, indifferent deliberation. Even this early in the morning he was dressed to perfection in a black swallow-tail coat and gaudy flowered vest and sharply creased pearl-grey trousers. He seemed to stare at Harland with complete disinterest.

Harland came to a stop about five feet from the two. He leaned an elbow on the bar, and, facing them, waited.

"I had begun to think you weren't going to come, Harland," he said in his quiet, detached way.

"I changed my mind," said Harland.

"Oh? And what made you change it?"

"I didn't have anything else to do so I thought I'd see what you've got on your mind."

Lowrie laid a short, direct look on Prentiss and the gunman, moving with elaborate casualness, filled his shot glass from the bottle on the bar and then, carrying the filled glass, moved to one of the tables. Harland watched him all the while. Prentiss set the glass down and then he pulled out a chair and seated himself. There was a deck of cards on the table and Prentiss shuffled these and then began to lay out a game of solitaire.

Harland turned his attention back to Lowrie to find the saloonman watching him intently. As Harland's glance swerved back, the avid interest faded from Lowrie's gaze and he looked bored once more. He crooked a finger at the bartender who brought an empty glass. Lowrie filled it from his bottle. Then he shoved the glass down the bar a little, towards Harland.

"This is really excellent bourbon, Harland. Wet your whistle."

"It's too early in the day for me."

Lowrie shrugged. He paused pensively as if he were considering something. Finally he said, "Well, we might as well get down to business, Harland. Will you step into my office?"

Without waiting for Harland's reply, Lowrie turned and started towards the back. Harland followed slowly. He put a deliberate glance on Prentiss, but the Dude appeared preoccupied with his solitaire. He sat hunched over his layout, studying it intently.

Lowrie stood in the entrance to his office, holding the door open, waiting for Harland. Harland passed inside. The room was plainly though expensively furnished. A mahogany rolltop desk was in one corner and in front of it was a swivel chair. In the centre of the room was a highly varnished table with four chairs around it. The far corner held a massive green safe with the name HAROLD LOWRIE stamped on it in gold leaf. The walls and ceiling were painted a light green and the only decoration was a framed picture of a Morgan horse.

Lowrie seated himself in the swivel chair and swung around so that he faced Harland. He motioned him to a seat at the table. As Harland sat down, Lowrie took a cigar box from his desk and proffered the Havanas to Harland. Harland shook his head.

Lowrie smiled faintly. "Are you afraid I'm trying to bribe you, Harland?" he asked softly. He took a cigar for himself and bit off the end.

"Don't mind me," Harland told Lowrie. "I was born suspicious. Since then, nothing has happened to make me change."

Lowrie struck a match and then he puffed loudly

on his cigar until he got it going to his satisfaction. He settled back in the swivel chair and pretended to be absorbed in the lighted end of the cigar.

"Harland, you've been trying to find out who it was that hired Jim Lancaster killed. I can tell you."

"I'm listening," Harland said as casually as he could.

Lowrie laid his glance on Harland. His dark eyes were cold and grave. "Before I name any names," Lowrie said quietly, "I want to point out to you that any violence on your part would be foolish. True, we're alone in here, but Dude is just outside the door. There is no other way out of this room."

Harland smiled thinly. "You have a lot of faith in Prentiss, haven't you?"

"He hasn't let me down yet."

"There is always a first time."

"I'm willing to take the chance." He paused again while his grave stare speculated on Harland. Then Lowrie eased forward in his chair. He brushed a fold of his coat aside, thus making the handle of the .45 at his hip readily available. "I won't beat about the bush, Harland, I had Lancaster killed!"

The faint, hard smile came to Harland's mouth again. He said nothing.

"You don't seem very impressed," Lowrie murmured.

"I'm not," Harland admitted.

"Why?"

"It's getting monotonous," said Harland. "First, Will Jordan sends for me and hands me a cock-and-bull story about having Lancaster killed. Then you send for me and tell me *you* had him killed. Both times Prentiss is around to make sure I don't get tough—as if Prentiss could prevent that!"

133

Now that he was convinced Harland was not going to get rough, Lowrie settled back in his chair again and puffed thoughtfully on his cigar. His eyes were alive with a brittle and bright calculation as they stared at Harland.

"Before you pass judgment on what I've said, why don't you hear me out, Harland?"

"I'm listening."

Lowrie frowned slightly as if in annoyance. Then he shrugged. "All right, Harland, I'll be frank with you. I put Jordan up to telling you that tale to cover up for me. Jordan owed me a little gambling debt which he had difficulty in squaring up, and I told him I'd cancel it in exchange for that favour. Jordan was leery of facing you himself with such a yarn. The only way I could get him to do it was to have Prentiss with him. Does that satisfy you, Harland?"

"Not quite," said Harland. "How come, after getting Jordan to lie in order to cover up for you, you turn around and tell me anyhow?"

Lowrie's mouth turned hard. "I've got to know if Lancaster's really dead. Is he, Harland?"

"How should I know?"

"Elliott hired you for the job, didn't he? Where did you kill and bury Lancaster, Harland?"

"I've never said I killed the man, have I?"

The fingers of Lowrie's left hand began to drum the top of his desk. Anger glinted in his eyes. "I paid good money to get rid of Lancaster. I want to know if the job was done."

"If you were so anxious to get rid of Lancaster, Lowrie, why didn't you let your fine, dependable boy, Dude, handle the job? He never lets you down, you know."

A muscle at the base of Lowrie's jaw kept twitching spasmodically. "I just told you I was trying to cover up for myself. Everybody knows Dude works for me. I didn't want to be tied in with Lancaster's death." He leaned forward in his chair. "Are you going to tell me, Harland?"

"I've got to be careful what I admit."

"Oh?" said Lowrie. He straightened in the chair as if a new comprehension of the matter had dawned on him. "Well, you've got nothing to be worried about with me. You can tell me. We're both in the same corral, Harland."

"Are we?" said Harland. "How do I know you ordered Lancaster killed? You haven't even given me a reason why you'd want him dead."

"All right," said Lowrie, settling back in the chair once more. He ground out the cigar with a gesture of annoyance. "I'll go along with you, Harland, just to prove to you that I'm being frank. I'm a businessman, Harland. I run this saloon to make a profit, not as a charitable enterprise. Any one is free and welcome to come in and try their luck at my gambling tables. If they win, they cash in their chips and I honour them with legitimate hard cash. If they lose I extend them credit. I expect them to pay up. Do you follow me?

"Jim Lancaster liked to gamble," Lowrie went on. "He began to lose and at first I extended him credit. When I figured he owed me enough, I cut his credit and told him to pay up. Lancaster said he didn't have the dinero." Lowrie spread his hands. "As you know, Harland, a gambling debt can't be collected in court. I couldn't very well let Lancaster get away with it. If I did that, then others would do the same. As long as they won, they'd expect me to pay off; when they lost, they'd borrow and never pay back." He shrugged. "So I had Lancaster killed as a warning to anyone who, in the future, might want to borrow money from me with the intention of never paying it back. I know it's harsh and brutal, Harland, but I'm a businessman. I can't afford to let sentiment interfere with business.''

"You're a man of extremes, aren't you, Lowrie?'' said Harland.

"What do you mean?''

"Will Jordan owes you a gambling debt and you let him square it by telling a simple lie. Jim Lancaster owes you a gambling debt and you have him killed. That's hardly fair, is it?''

Lowrie sat silent for a while, his dark gaze never leaving Harland's face. The fingers of Lowrie's left hand began to drum against the silver buckle of his shell belt.

Finally, Lowrie said, "You've been out to Bridlebit, Harland. I also know you've been out to Quarter Circle L.'' He paused as if to let Harland digest this. "I let Jordan off easy because I wanted him to ask for more credit.'' Lowrie's eyes were hard, inscrutable slits. "Bridlebit is a juicy plum. I've had my eyes on it for a long time. Quarter Circle L isn't worth the price of a wind-broken horse. In other words, Jordan had security and Lancaster didn't.''

"I don't think so,'' said Harland. "Lancaster could have paid you easy.''

"Oh?''

"There's one thing I believe about Lancaster,'' Harland continued. "He held up that Border Pacific train. Even one third of a hundred thousand dollars should have been more than enough to pay you off.''

"I'm glad you brought that up,'' said Lowrie. He seemed anxious to explain. "Lancaster had the money from that stick-up and he offered to square his bill with me. I turned him down. Do you know why, Harland?''

"Why?"

"I was not going to get mixed up in it. I told Lancaster that. I told him I was not going to accept any money from any hold-up and run the risk of being accused as an accomplice. Can't you see, Harland? If Lancaster were picked up and brought to trial, a smart lawyer could dig up the fact that he owed me money. He could maybe even convince a jury I put Lancaster up to robbing a train just to pay me off.'' He shook his head emphatically. "No, sir. I was not getting mixed up in that B.P. job."

"So you decided to have Lancaster killed."

"That's right."

"Why did you have Jordan killed?"

For the moment Lowrie's mouth hung open. Then the astonishment passed and he smiled derisively. "Come now, Harland, you're smarter than that. Jordan's no good to me dead. In fact, the man who killed Jordan did me a great disfavour. I had planned to use Jordan to get my hands on Bridlebit. Now that he's dead, I can't plan on that any more.'' He was still amused. "Besides, why would I want to kill Jordan? Because I was afraid he'd tell you I had ordered Lancaster's death? Haven't I told you that myself?"

"Why was Jordan killed then?"

"I can't say exactly. Jordan liked to drink and he was always getting into trouble. Maybe he insulted the wrong man when he was drunk or maybe he fooled around with the wrong man's wife." Lowrie shrugged. "Anyway, he did something to get someone mad enough at him to put a slug in his back. But it wasn't me, Harland."

"All right," said Harland. "I'm convinced." He rose to his feet.

"Are you leaving?" asked Lowrie. His voice became a murmur. "You know, you haven't told me yet if Lancaster's dead."

"That's right," said Harland. He stood staring down at Lowrie.

"You're not getting away with it," said Lowrie. His face seemed paler than usual.

"Getting away with what?"

Lowrie ignored the query. "Who sent you here, Harland?"

"I came on my own."

"Why?"

Harland thought it over. Then he said, "You wouldn't understand, Lowrie." He meant it.

Lowrie's chest rose and fell. He was patently putting out a great effort to hold himself in check. "I've been frank with you, Harland, because I thought that then you'd be frank with me. I've told you everything yet you refuse to tell me one little thing in return."

"All you've done, Lowrie, is muddy the creek."

Lowrie's lips were thin white stripes of anger. "You've come here for one of two reasons, Harland. The first of them could be that hundred thousand from the stick-up. Is that what you're after?"

"I'll answer that after you give me the second reason."

Lowrie laughed in Harland's face. "I'll let you guess about that one. If you guess wrong, I won't tell you. It'll be something for you to worry about."

"Maybe," said Harland, "but I won't worry half as much as you. After all, Lowrie, you still don't know whether Lancaster is dead, and if he still happens to be alive, you've admitted wanting him killed." He smiled faintly and started for the door. "You're wrong about me, Lowrie. You're the one who has to do the worrying."

Chapter Thirteen

Night came to Edenville. Shadow crawled over the town, filling in the ample spaces between the buildings, and lights started to twinkle in the windows.

Up in his room in the Lamar House, Dan Harland lay in darkness. Twilight had come and then the shadows had thickened in the room, but Harland did not rise from his bed to light the lantern. He was trying to sleep, though he knew it was no use.

He was thinking of all the things that had happened to him since he had come into the Stalwarts. He was taking the incidents one by one and examining them and then trying to fit them together. However, he could not achieve a pattern that made sense to him. He could not arrive at any final, definite conclusion.

Harland spent a long time deciding what to do next. Weighing all the knowledge, both worthless and genuine, that he had picked up during his stay here, he finally began to see something that had escaped his comprehension up till now. From his actions, Lancaster had indicated that he knew he had been marked for death. To Harland's way of thinking, there was just one person who could have or would have warned Lancaster.

Harland's heart was beating with a new, eager excitement as he rose from his bed and prepared to go outside.

The Ace of Diamonds was going full blast. It was the first of the month and it had been payday at the ranches in the valley, and the cowhands were busy getting rid of their money before it burned holes in their pockets.

The place was loud with laughter and joviality, and the boisterous voices drowned out all other sounds. The piano player and the singer were doing their best, but they could not hope to compete with the customers who cared little if they had music and song.

The atmosphere suited Harland to perfection. No one seemed to care what was going on about him and Harland figured he'd have almost more privacy here than in a private room. Moreover, he would not look as conspicuous.

He peered through the smoke-hazed barroom, but could not spy the woman named Lily. She might be otherwise occupied, Harland thought, and so he elbowed a place for himself at the crowded bar and ordered a whisky.

He had been there only a couple of minutes when he felt someone crowding in beside him. It was Rose.

"Well, well," she said, "if it ain't the handsome, bashful cowboy. Why've you been avoiding me, honey?"

Harland grinned a little and said nothing. Cacophonous noise pounded at him from all directions. Rose squeezed herself harder against him.

"Aren't you gonna buy me a drink, handsome?"

"I was waiting for you to ask me," said Harland. "You're so shy about it."

"Don't go getting funny with me," she snarled, but when Harland beckoned the bartender and he brought Rose a glass, she dismissed her temper and smiled at him again. "Let's me and you have a good time, cowboy," she murmured.

"I don't have the time right now," said Harland. "Is Lily around?"

"You and that goddamn Lily," growled Rose. "What you so hot about her for?"

Harland grinned and chucked her chin. "You're cute when you're mad," he said, trying not to wince as he spoke. He caught a whiff of her breath as she belched. "You've been snorting out of the wrong bottle, honey."

"So what?"

"Ace won't like it."

Rose made a very unladylike observation about Ace. "I'm sure not gonna make much money with you, cowboy," she said. Her glass was in front of her, but she reached over and grabbed Harland's shot and downed it with one expert swallow. She belched again and winked at him. "Thanks for the drink, cowboy. Drop in again sometime when you're feeling reckless."

With that, she turned to the cowpuncher beside her and began to promote again. With a wry grin, Harland stepped away from the bar. He began working through the crowd, seeking Lily.

He got to the back, beside the raised platform

where the piano and the singer were still bravely carrying on, and he saw Lily coming down from upstairs. She did not see him, and had started past him when Harland reached out and caught her arm.

"How about having a drink with me, Lily?" he said.

She turned with that mechanical smile, but when she saw who it was the grin blanched on her face. Harland did not let go of her arm. He gripped it a little tighter and steered her towards the bar. He reached between two customers for the drinks and then he put an arm around Lily and steered her towards a table. He sat down beside her, his arm still around her. He hoped he looked very amorous to anyone who might care to watch.

The smile kept going and coming on Lily's face. "What do you want, Harland?" she asked. She sounded worried.

"I want to talk to you about Jim Lancaster," Harland said quietly. He had his mouth close to Lily's ear, hoping that this might be interpreted as affection. He felt Lily go rigid beneath the arm he had clasped about her, but that painted smile stayed on her face. "You were sweet on him, weren't you?"

"You crazy, Harland?"

"You liked him," Harland persisted.

"I liked him just like anybody who spends money on me."

"It was more than just business with Lancaster."

She tried to get out from under his arm. "I don't want to talk with you any more. Find yourself another girl, Harland."

Harland's hold tightened. "Should I tell Lowrie who warned Lancaster he was going to be killed?" he hissed in her ear.

He felt her go limp. The fight fled from her. Fright lurked deep in her eyes as she stared up at him. "Don't forget your smile," he told her.

But she didn't put it on. She looked at him gravely, her small mouth tight with fear. "What do you want?" she asked in a hoarse whisper. "Didn't you kill Jim? Why don't you leave me alone?"

"I'm your friend, Lily."

"Ha!" she said.

"I'm on your side. I'm out to square for Lancaster. Don't you want him squared up?"

Her eyes worked on his face as if they were trying to get beneath the surface to find out what was going on in his head. "How dumb do you think I am, Harland? You were hired to kill Jim, weren't you? Yet you say you're going to square for him. Don't make me laugh."

Bitterness edged Harland's tone. "I'm a hired killer. I work for whoever pays me. Maybe someone is paying me to square for Lancaster. Have you ever thought of that? Killing for pay is my business."

She kept staring at him as if she could not make up her mind to believe him. He went on urgently, "Don't you want to help me square for Lancaster? I know you loved him. Elliott didn't mean anything to you. It was Lancaster for you, wasn't it? Elliott spilled to you what had been planned for Lancaster and you passed the tip on to him. Who planned that for Lancaster, Lily?"

She shook her head mutely. Her eyes were wide with terror.

"You're going to tell me, Lily. Who ordered Lancaster's death?"

"I—I can't tell you here."

"No one's listening. No one has any idea what we're talking about."

"No. Not here."

"We can go upstairs then."

"I don't want to be seen alone with you."

"Then tell me here. Whisper it in my ear."

He could feel her whole body trembling. Her eyes batted with fright and indecision. Finally she said, "Come out to my place where I room. It's the last house on your right on Fremont Street. I won't be through here until about four in the morning. Come there about a half-hour later. No one will be up to see you at that hour. I—I'm scared, Harland, and I don't want to be seen with you in case something goes wrong."

"Nothing will go wrong."

"How can you be sure?"

"Because I'm killing whoever you name!"

She looked at him gravely for a while. Then she shook her head slowly. "No, Harland, you'll never do that."

It was just getting light in the sky above the mountain tops. A thin, pale band of light limned the ragged crests of the Stalwarts in the east.

The night clerk of the Lamar House dozed at his desk and Harland passed through the lobby outside without being noticed. He struck out afoot across the sleeping town. He came to Fremont Street and started along that.

He was positive no one had seen him as he came to the last house on Fremont Street. By now the first greyness of dawn had begun to reach down in the valley. The world started to take hazy shape about Harland. There was an almost unreal quality in the somnolent huddling of the houses in this the first pale beginning of the day.

The last house on Fremont Street was a decrepit affair. It appeared to have been hurriedly thrown together as if whoever had constructed it had had no intention of living in it very long. It was unpainted and the boards were greyish-black in colour from the wear and tear of wind and rain and sun.

Like all the other houses Harland had passed, it was dark. However, this did not strike Harland as out of the ordinary. He remembered Lily's fear and he was not over surprised that she was not showing a light.

It was not until he reached the door that the first sick feeling of dread hit Harland. The door was wide open. All was darkness beyond the gaping door, just a solid mass of concealing black, thick with a foreboding evil. Harland pulled his .44 before he stepped inside.

He did not go all the way in. Just over the threshold, he stepped to the left with his back up hard against the wall, and he stood like that a minute, gun in hand, heart thudding slowly, leadenly inside him, while his eyes accustomed themselves to the darkness.

After a moment, he realised he was the only one in this house so far as living people went. There was a film of sweat on his forehead as his eyes began to make out the shape of things.

Not far from Harland there was a bed, and on the bed was something that did not move. After watching it for a couple of minutes, Harland became convinced it would never move of its own accord again.

He could hear the shallow sound of his breathing as he moved up to the bed. There was the scent of lilacs in his nose, and something else which he could not immediately place. He remembered this was Lily's choice of perfume, and he knew what to expect even before he struck the match.

The small, flickering light was feeble, but it sufficed. Lily lay horribly contorted in death as if she had fought desperately for the last, final gulp of air she had never got. Her eyes bulged and her round features were a bluish red and her mouth still gaped as if she were yet waiting for the next breath which would never come for her.

Harland waved out the match and stepped back. For a while he stood there, with the clammy feel of death crawling all over him, trying to grasp that which his mind was screaming at him. At first, he could not conceive what it was. All he knew was that there was something in and about this room which should have a meaning for him.

At first, he was aware only of Lily's dead form on the bed and the sad, lingering smell of her perfume which seemed to go on living even though she was dead. Then it came to Harland that it wasn't only the smell of lilacs.

There was also the faint, barely perceptible odour of cologne.

It was two o'clock in the afternoon before Harland found Dude Prentiss. It was Harland's third trip to the Ace of Diamonds that day and, as he pushed through the swing doors, he half expected this one to be fruitless just like the other two. But his glance instantly picked out Prentiss.

The Dude was sitting alone at a table, engrossed in a game of solitaire. He looked clean and refreshed as if he had woken up perhaps an hour ago and had washed and eaten and was now relaxing, at peace with both himself and the world. The sight infuriated Harland.

He pulled out a chair at the table next to Prentiss. He turned the chair around and sat down straddling it but facing Prentiss. Harland's left arm was hooked above the back of the chair. His right hand rested on his thigh, not far from the handle of his .44.

Prentiss stared at that hand a while, then he raised his glance and looked thoughtfully at Harland's face. What he interpreted there drew some of the arrogance out of Prentiss's eyes. One corner of his mouth curled as if he were going to speak, but then he changed his mind and with a slight shrug turned his attention back to his game.

Harland watched in silence. The game stumped Prentiss and he gathered up the cards, shuffled them and laid out another game. He made several plays, then stopped in annoyance and put the deck down. His chair complained as he scraped it around a little so that he could better observe Harland.

"Something on your mind, Harland?" the Dude asked coldly.

"No."

"What you sitting there for?"

"I'm just killing—time," murmured Harland. He pointed with a finger of his left hand. "Black six on red seven."

"There's a deck on your table," snapped Prentiss. "If you want to play, deal a game for yourself."

"My, my, what a temper."

The Dude regarded Harland with slitted eyes. "What are you leading up to, Harland?"

"Nothing."

"I know better than that. What have you come here for?"

"I like the smell of cologne."

Prentiss flushed, but he did not look as if the meaning had registered on him. For a moment Harland feared he was wrong.

The Dude returned to his game. Harland went on watching. The Dude's lips were thin and pale and pinched in tight against his teeth. He appeared to be trying to ignore Harland very strongly. Harland did not move. He just kept looking.

This game, too, stumped Prentiss. He gathered up the cards and shuffled. He dealt another layout on the table and he played hunched over this one, his nose not more than six inches from the cards, trying to appear as if he was all wrapped up in the game and was entirely oblivious of anything else going on. But he missed a couple of plays and gave up before he had to.

He swept a hand over the table, breaking up the solitaire layout in a fit of extreme irritation. He turned hot, angry eyes on Harland.

"Do you have to sit there and watch?"

"Is there something that says I can't?"

Prentiss shoved his chair back a little more and straightened out his right leg so that the pearl handle of his Colt swung free. His right hand dropped out of sight below his thigh.

Harland's heart quickened. He did not want it yet. He was deriving too much pleasure out of thinking about it. He had never before in his life known any pleasure at the thought of killing, but he knew that sensation now and he liked it and he did not want it to end too quick.

"What have you got on your mind, Harland?" the Dude asked. His tone was gelid.

149

"You don't have to be so jumpy, Dude. I'm your friend."

"I'm not jumpy, and you're no friend of mine," said Prentiss with a sneer.

"Oh, but I am," Harland said gently. "If I wasn't your friend, I wouldn't be telling you this." He lowered his voice confidentially. "A man in your line of work, Dude, should never use cologne. The smell stays on for quite a while, you know."

This time it opened the corral gate in the Dude's mind. His face slacked in shocked surprise and his mouth hung open for an instant and a wild glint of fear paraded through his eyes. Then he recovered and pulled his chair back up to the table and began to pick up the scattered cards. "I don't know what you're talking about," he growled. He shuffled the cards and started another layout. His fingers trembled ever so slightly as he laid the cards on the table.

Harland said nothing. He went on watching Prentiss.

The Dude did not even start this game. He no sooner had the layout down than he swept that hand over the table once more. This time some of the cards went flying off on the floor. With a muffled curse, Prentiss jerked to his feet and stalked up to the bar.

He called loudly for whisky and he was lifting the glass to his lips when he saw Harland coming up beside him. The Dude tossed the drink off angrily and whirled to face Harland. Rage made a grimace out of the Dude's mouth.

Harland never took his eyes off Prentiss. With a finger of his left hand he beckoned the bartender and ordered a beer. When the brew was placed before him Harland did not touch it. He did not even glance at it. He went on staring at Prentiss.

"What the hell's the matter with you today?" snarled the Dude. There was a crack in his voice.

"Nothing's the matter," said Harland. "I feel fine."

"What you tailing after me for?"

"I'm trying to remember where else I've smelled that cologne."

The Dude blanched. His tongue darted out and dabbed at his lips. He started to sweat. "Why don't you make sense? I don't know what the hell you're talking about."

"I'm making sense," said Harland quietly. "For you I'm making sense."

The Dude poised his right hand above the handle of his .45. "You looking for trouble?" he snarled, trying to bluster out of it.

Harland's eyes became slits of ice. "Go right ahead, Dude," he murmured.

"You've been pasturing on loco weed," Dude told Harland. He turned from Harland to the bar and ordered another slug. The Dude tossed this one off swiftly. Then, turning his back on Harland, Prentiss started for the door.

Harland went after him. The Dude pretended to be unconcerned. Outside, he paused on the edge of the board walk and placed his hands in his pockets and whistled a little tune. Harland just leaned against the front wall of the Ace of Diamonds until the Dude tired of his act of nonchalance and stepped off into the street. Harland followed.

By the time he had reached the street in front of Masterson's Mercantile, Prentiss could no longer contain his anger. He whirled around, crouching, his mouth contorted with wrathful insufferableness.

"Goddam you," he cried. "Quit following me around!"

"I finally remembered," Harland said quietly. "I smelled cologne on Fremont Street early this morning. You ever been on Fremont Street, Dude?"

Prentiss's chest heaved with fury. The corners of his mouth pulled down, he was all carried away by his wrath. "You think you're smart, don't you, Harland?" he snarled. "Well, you're not quite smart enough."

A moment more Prentiss hesitated. Then his hand darted for his gun. He was fast. The sun barely had time to catch the ornate silver inlays that covered the weapon before it was roaring. But the slugs came nowhere near Harland.

Harland's first shot took the Dude in the chest a fraction of a second before he fired. The force and shock of it jarred him and the silver barrel of his Colt tilted towards the sky as he pressed the trigger. The second slug took Prentiss in the belly and he doubled up with a hoarse scream. His .45 blasted again, but this time the barrel was pointing at the ground and the bullet only kicked up dust. Harland's third shot smashed into the Dude's brain and he made no sound after this one. He dropped as if his legs had suddenly been cut out from under him. The force with which he hit the ground raised a small swirl of dust. It was the only thing that moved about the Dude.

Mingled with the acrid odour of black gunpowder smoke was the faint, cloying scent of cologne.

Chapter Fourteen

Early the next morning, Harland went to Beeson's and got his bay. He saddled up and rode out of Edenville. He had had a good night, the best sleep since he had come to the Stalwarts, and this disturbed him a little. Killing Prentiss had not bothered Harland a bit. On the contrary, it had made him feel good and he wondered if this was the beginning of his final fall into that degree of rottenness where killing was only a casual thing. The thought of this chilled the back of Harland's neck.

He headed for that branch of the Stalwarts where Quarter Circle L lay, with a sort of eagerness. He told himself he was going there because he was convinced that was the only remaining place where he could hope to pick up any more information to aid his quest. There was nothing fruitful left in Edenville. Lily was dead and so was Prentiss. Lowrie most certainly would be of no help and at best would only repeat what he had already told Harland. So Quarter Circle L remained the only source of information.

Harland would not admit that most of the reason for the excitement in his heart was Lorraine Lancaster. He had not seen her for several days, but that had not helped any in taking her out of his mind. Despite the feeling of guilt and wrongness, he had decided not to fight it any more. The thing had shaped up like that and he would accept it as it was. He was powerless to do otherwise.

The bay mounted to high ground. The day grew increasingly warmer and Harland removed his denim jacket and tied it behind the cantle of his saddle. The distance to Quarter Circle L shortened and over Harland there crawled a cold presentiment of evil.

He tried to shrug the sensation from him but it would not go. It seemed to cling to him with a morbid, unclean tenacity. He tried analysing why he should feel this way. Perhaps it was due to the guilt he experienced in loving Lorraine Lancaster, but something in his mind told him it was more than that. He had a sudden premonition that the source of this emotion lay in the reason for Lancaster's death. The exact nature of the matter, however, escaped him.

It was around midday that the rider suddenly appeared ahead of Harland. Harland, as usual, had been making his way through the more open reaches of ground. To his left the land rose sharply in a barren, greyish slope that was beginning to be eroded by wind and water. The top of the rise was covered by a grove of nut pines and the rider appeared out of these.

He popped into sight and then sent his mount sliding on its haunches down the steep slope, raising a cloud of dust and starting a miniature slide of sand and gravel that preceded him down the incline. Harland reined in his bay and waited. The rider was Mitch Antrim.

The bay whinnied and Antrim's sorrel answered, and then there was only the soft plop of the sorrel's hooves as it approached at a walk. Ten feet away, Antrim reined in the sorrel. He dismounted. Turning his back on Harland, Antrim dug in the roll behind his cantle and came up with a bottle. He lifted the bottle to his mouth and drank deeply. Then he returned the bottle to the cantle without offering any to Harland.

Harland was tired of sitting in the kak and so he stepped down from the bay. He did not approach Antrim. Harland waited there to see what Antrim had on his mind.

With his bottle put away, Antrim turned. He appeared a bit unsteady on his feet and he put out a hand and caught the sorrel's mane to steady himself. The redhead's face was strangely grave this day. There was none of the reckless humour or brooding regret. His face was flushed and he was apparently drunk but his eyes were cold and hard.

Finally Antrim spoke. "It's a nice day for riding, isn't it, amigo?" He did not sound too friendly.

"It sure is," agreed Harland. He could hear the short, swift pounding of his heart. There was a strange feeling in the palms of his hands.

"You going anywhere in particular?"

"Just riding," said Harland.

"You wouldn't be going to Quarter Circle L, would you, amigo?"

A poignant regret filled Harland. He could not help

155

remembering how Antrim felt about Lorraine Lancaster. It made Harland rather sad.

"I'm sorry, Mitch," he said.

"You don't have to be sorry about me," Antrim flared. However, he quickly caught himself. Drawing a deep breath, he went on more quietly, "You've been in the Stalwarts for some time now, Harland. Isn't it about time you left?"

Something began to cry in Harland's brain. "I don't think I'll be here much longer, Mitch," he said.

Antrim paused. He seemed to be considering what Harland had said. After a while, Antrim said, "Then you're about done?"

Harland nodded.

The flush went slowly out of Antrim's cheeks. They turned grey. He lifted a hand and rubbed it against his mouth. "That means you've found what you were looking for. Is that right, amigo?"

"Just about."

"Would you mind telling me?"

Harland stared at Antrim with narrowed eyes. "Where do you come into this, Mitch?"

"Answer me first and then I'll tell you."

"What do you want to know?"

"The reason you came to the Stalwarts," said Antrim.

"I'm looking for the man who ordered the death of Jim Lancaster."

"Then Lancaster's dead?"

"That's one thing I won't tell you, Mitch."

"All right," said Antrim. He seemed to speak most carefully. "Have you found your man yet, amigo?"

"Not yet."

"Have you any idea who he is?"

"I'm getting there," said Harland.

Antrim sucked in his breath deeply. His face grew still paler. "When you find your man, amigo, what are you going to do?"

"I'm going to kill him!"

"Well, amigo," Antrim said softly, "that man is me!"

The world seemed to shatter. Those other admissions of Jordan and Lowrie, Harland had taken with a concession to doubt. He was trying to take this one the same way, but it would not come like that.

Resentment seemed to flare in Antrim's eyes as Harland made no attempt to speak. "Doesn't it make sense to you, amigo?" he cried. "Can't you see why it was? I wanted Lorraine. Goddam it, don't you want her, too? I couldn't kill Lancaster myself and expect to have her then, could I? I had to hire it done and I had to keep myself covered up so she'd never catch on." He was sweating profusely. "Isn't that enough for you, amigo?"

Harland stood there stunned. His mind kept trying to tell him something but he could not seem to understand the language. He could only stare with hurt in his eyes at Antrim.

The agony drained out of Antrim's features. His voice turned gentle. "Well, amigo, that doesn't give us much of a choice, does it?"

Harland knew what Antrim meant. It was this that Harland had feared all along, it was this that put the ache in his heart. He could only stand there and wait, his mind rebelling silently, futilely against it. There was no use talking. All the talking had been done. It was time for something more definite and decisive.

He watched, appalled, as Antrim's mouth tightened. He watched the slow shifting of Antrim's hand to a spot just above the handle of his .45. He watched until Antrim's eyes suddenly distended and his hand dipped. Then Harland drew and fired.

He fired just this once for he had Antrim beat and there was need for no more bullets. The .45 in Antrim's hand never even went off. The slug crashed into his chest, sending him back up against his sorrel. He put out a hand to grab the sorrel somewhere, but the horse, frightened, wheeled away and Antrim went sprawling on his back.

For half a minute Harland stood there, frozen, dully watching the smoke curling out of the bore of his .44. There seemed to be something reminiscent about this. He could not help remembering how it had been with Lancaster, only Lancaster had actually beaten Harland to the draw. With Antrim it differed only in this respect. Maybe Antrim had not been much of a hand with a gun, or maybe he had not tried very hard. Of this Harland could not be sure.

Now Harland stirred himself and walked ahead slowly until he stood above Antrim. The redhead lay with eyes closed, breathing heavily, his chest rising and falling with the labour of each breath. His face held a waxen pallor and this and the blood pumping out of the wound in Antrim's chest told Harland the redhead did not have much longer to go.

Antrim sensed that Harland was standing there. His eyes fluttered and opened. They were luminous with pain, but their stare held steady and direct on Harland.

Harland holstered his weapon. He built a smoke, all the while not meeting Antrim's gaze, and then he dropped to his knees and stuck the cigarette in Antrim's mouth. Antrim began to search feebly in the pockets of his vest.

Harland fished out a match and struck it and held the flame to Antrim's smoke. Antrim took a puff of it and exhaled. "Thanks, amigo," he murmured.

He lay there quietly, drawing now and then on his smoke. After a moment, his eyes began to look past Harland as if into a great distance. Antrim lay like that for quite a while. He appeared to be absorbed in some secret thought. It was as if he were making a summation of all the things he had ever done. At the end of a while, his mouth took on a tiny, bitter twist. Then he seemed to glimpse the nearness of death and a bit of panic flared in his eyes and they pulled back to the present and began searching Harland's face.

"You understand how it was, don't you, amigo?" asked Antrim. He spoke only with the greatest of effort. Tiny globules of sweat stood out on his forehead and upper lip. The perspiration seemed glued there, the glistening beads of moisture did not run. "I—I went crazy. I thought if Lancaster was out of the way, then maybe I could have Lorraine. Hell, I've loved her all my life. There's never been anyone else for me. Do you understand why I did it?"

"I understand, Mitch."

Antrim's glance moved beyond Harland again. Antrim seemed to speak now more to himself. "I never blamed her for marrying Lancaster. I've never been any damn good. All my life I've been no good. A man's got to do something sometime. He's got to do something good. Isn't that right, amigo?" His eyes swivelled back to Harland. His hand began to paw urgently at Harland's arm.

"That's right, Mitch."

He caught Antrim's hand and squeezed it. That seemed to soothe Antrim. He lay quietly again. His eyes began to look into the past once more.

"I don't know why I ever was like this," he said thoughtfully. "I never was one for hard work. I liked the stuff in bottles and jugs. To get that stuff, I've cheated at cards. I've rustled cows. I've done a lot of low, dirty things." He began to sweat hard. Now the glittering beads broke loose and channelled down his cheeks. "It's tough for a man to die without having done one right thing. Do you understand, amigo?" The focus of his eyes was on Harland now. "I've tried to square up for all the rotten things I've done in my life. Do you think I've squared for them, amigo?"

Harland nodded. He could not speak past the obstruction that had suddenly lodged in his throat. He was finally beginning to see how it had really been. He was beginning to see this now when it was too late to do anything about Antrim.

"I don't want to leave any unfinished business behind me," Antrim went on with a weak urgency. "I want the herd tallied up to the last head. That's why I'm telling you again, amigo, that it was me who wanted Jim Lancaster dead."

"I believe you, Mitch." Harland could not say anything else.

A look of relief and peace came into Antrim's features. "Then you're all done in the Stalwarts? Then there's nothing else to keep you here?"

Harland nodded. He did not trust himself to speak.

"Then you'll be going home, amigo?"

"I'll be going home, Mitch."

Antrim smiled. He held up his right hand and Harland took it. "No hard feelings, amigo," murmured Antrim. "No hard feelings at all."

Once more his gaze moved beyond Harland. Antrim lay like that a long while, looking up at the sky, smiling as if with a deep inner satisfaction, seeing something that to him must have been pretty good. He went on staring, unblinking, until it dawned on Harland that Antrim was not seeing anything any more.

Chapter Fifteen

There was a small cutback not far off and Harland dragged Antrim's body over there. Then he crawled up on the bank and caved down as much dirt as he could so that Antrim was completely covered. Next Harland picked up all the loose stones he could find in the vicinity until he had made a small mound above where Mitch Antrim was buried. The pile of stones served both as a monument and as a deterrent to any scavengers. When he was through, Harland paused a moment beside Antrim's grave and thought about what the man had done. There was no need for words, Harland felt. The manner of Antrim's death spoke more eloquently for him than any prayers or readings out of books.

Harland had just turned away from the grave when the rider hove into sight. Harland's first reaction was to whip out his .44, but then recognition came and

Harland slowly returned his gun to its holster. He walked ahead to meet the rider, who was Glennis Jordan.

She reined in the palomino and her glance went past Harland to the pile of stones. Her face looked grave and even severe, there was an odd, irreconcilable hurt in the tight squinting of her eyes. She stared at the mound a while. Then her look averted and rested coolly on Harland.

"Who is it, Harland?" she asked quietly.

"Mitch Antrim." The name sounded like the tolling of a requiem in Harland's ears. He felt hollow and inadequate inside.

The girl said, "Oh!" That was all.

Harland's eyes narrowed slightly as he stared up at her. "Did you know him?"

"I never knew him personally. I used to see him around Edenville and other places, but I didn't know him to speak to him." Her gaze rested cool and speculative on him. She paused and crossed her hands on the saddlehorn. After a moment, she said, "Is he the one who killed my brother?"

Harland shook his head.

"Was it Prentiss then?"

"You know about Prentiss?"

"You killed him where everyone could see it, didn't you? Word of a thing like that gets around pretty fast." She drew a deep breath. "It was Prentiss who killed my brother, wasn't it?"

"I can't tell you for sure. I think Prentiss was the one. In fact, I'm pretty positive of it, but I have no definite proof."

"Why did you kill Prentiss?"

Harland opened his mouth to speak, then closed it abruptly. "You wouldn't understand," he said.

"But I would understand," she said with a low fierce vehemence that startled him. She leaned forward in the saddle her face thrusting down at him. He could see the ugly virulence in her eyes. "I understand perfectly, Harland, because I want to kill myself. Once I couldn't understand why there had to be violence in the world, but that was before Will was killed. Now I want to kill. I want to kill with my own hands."

Harland could scarcely believe his ears but, looking at her, he could see that she meant every word. His glance moved from her hate-ridden, purposeful face to the stock of the Winchester sticking out of the saddle boot. His mind felt chilled and stunned.

"Don't talk like that," he told her sternly.

"How do you want me to talk?" she flared. "Do you want me to give out with cheap, flighty gossip? Do you want me to tell you what lovely weather we've been having?" Her voice broke. "He was my brother. He was all the family I had left in the world. He was shiftless and lazy and plain no good, but he was my brother and I loved him more than anything in the world." Moisture came to her eyes but she brushed it away angrily. "I haven't forgotten what you told me a few days ago. You feel you have to kill, Harland, even though you hate the thought of killing, but there's nothing you can do about it. Can't somebody else feel the same way? Can't I feel the same way?"

It sickened Harland to hear her talking like this. He knew it was the product of her grief and loneliness and he sympathised with her, but he did not want to hear her talking with such a vicious purpose. She was young and pretty. She should have only thoughts of womanly things and frivolity—not of violence.

"Prentiss is dead," he pointed out to her gently. "It's all over with. There's nothing left for you to do, Glennis, but to forget."

"Prentiss is dead all right," she said, "but Prentiss was only acting for someone else. Who hired Prentiss, Harland?"

"I don't know."

"Don't lie to me, Harland."

He felt himself get angry and sick inside at the thought of what lay ahead. He walked up until he stood beside the palomino. Harland reached up and took one of her hands. She made no move to withdraw it. It felt slim and cold in Harland's grip.

"Listen, Glennis," he said earnestly, "leave it up to me, won't you? I'll take care of it. It's a job for me, for a killer. Don't ever let me hear you say again that you want to kill. I know what it's like. It isn't the killings that you detest that are bad. It's the ones that you enjoy."

She stared soberly down at him. "Do you know who you have to kill, Harland?"

"I have a pretty good idea."

"Won't you tell me?"

"No."

"Not even if I promise not to do anything about it?"

He shook his head. "It's something that's rotten and evil all the way through. It's not anything for you to get mixed up in. I'll take care of it, Glennis. I'll square for your brother at the same time I square for Lancaster. This is a job that can be done only by an out-and-out killer."

The glint in her eyes seemed to soften. "You're not that, Harland," she whispered, "not an out-and-out killer. I don't care what kind of name you've got. I know you better than that.''

He smiled a little. "Thanks," he murmured.

Her hand squeezed his. "I just want to tell you this, Harland. Please don't go into it not caring at all whether you come out alive or dead. Try to keep on living, won't you?''

He put the foreboding of evil from him and smiled again. "I'll try," he said. "You can bet I'll try...."

Harland reached Quarter Circle L as the sun was going down. He reined in the bay as he emerged from the pines and, for a while, sat in his kak, observing the layout ahead. He thought he had seen something up past the house, but the thing had been so slight and phantasmal that, after a moment, he dismissed it as a product of his own uneasiness and disquietude.

Still he sat there on the bay, intensely vigilant, while he fashioned a smoke and lighted it. The scene ahead of him was one redolent of peace and charm. With the sun gone down behind the mountain, the shadows began to thicken. The land took on a sense of restfulness. For a little while, hate and greed and violence seemed like distant, alien things to Harland. Then he told himself grimly that he knew better and, the spell broken, he urged the bay ahead.

He rounded the corrals and saw in one of them the pinto that Lorraine Lancaster rode, as well as a big hammer-head roan and a grulla mare. All three horses carried the Quarter Circle L brand. Three horses trotted up against the corral bars and whinned as Harland's bay passed. The sound of this carried up to the house and a moment later Lorraine Lancaster appeared.

She stepped out of the door to the ground and stopped, watching Harland riding up. He reined in the bay and dismounted. He took two more drags to finish his smoke and then he dropped it and ground it out with the toe of his boot.

She stood there silently, answering his stare and study of her with one of her own. She looked strangely appealing and desirable to Harland, and he felt the old want rise in him. He told himself it was no good for him, but in the same instant he recognised the futility of trying to fight it. She still stirred him such as no woman ever had. Even now, she still had that effect on him, and Harland felt a sullen resentment edge into his brain.

Like all the other times that he had seen her, she was wearing men's clothing. This time she was wearing a plain black flannel shirt which was open enough at the neck to reveal the first faint rise of her breasts. The Levi's she had on were clean but faded and worn. On her feet she wore high-heeled riding boots but no spurs. Around her waist she had a shell-belt and the holstered Bisley .38-40. Harland wondered that she should be wearing the gun at home.

The wall of silence continued between them. Harland did not know how to begin. He kept remembering the last time he had been here and the guilt and the contempt he had felt for himself. He supposed it might be the same with her. She watched him gravely and, it seemed, with a well-concealed wariness.

The idea of just standing there silently annoyed Harland. He moved up past her and sat down on the stoop and began to build another smoke. When he was finished with it, he discovered that he did not want it. So he dropped it into his shirt pocket that held the Bull Durham and papers.

He lifted his glance and stared up at her. She was the one who broke the silence.

"I was beginning to think you were never going to come around again, Harland," she said quietly.

"I started to come a few days ago," he said, "but then I turned back."

"Why?"

He averted his gaze from her and stared over the pines into the darkening twilight. He shrugged and said nothing.

"Is it because of the way you feel about me?" she asked throatily.

"Perhaps. I don't know for sure."

"Why did you come here now?"

He turned his glance upward and stared at her again. She had come ahead a step. She stood there, tall and grave, gazing down at him with a bold intensity in those light blue eyes.

"I wish I could stay away," he murmured softly and frankly.

"Why?"

Harland knew why, but he was not going to tell her. He would never tell her. It made him sad and bitter and sick, all mixed up together, inside. He shrugged.

"Is it because you killed Jim?" she persisted when he did not answer. "Is that what you've got on your mind? Is that what's holding you back?"

"I never said I killed your husband."

"I know you never did. Won't you even tell me if he's dead?"

"I don't know," said Harland.

A look of extreme irritation and insufferableness came into her face, but it was swiftly gone. She came ahead another step so that she towered above him. A moment she stood like that, then she dropped to her knees beside him. The sharpness of her stare was an almost palpable thing.

"Don't you—like me any more, Harland?" she asked just above a whisper.

He looked at her hard. He told himself he was not going to let it get him this time. He told himself he was going to be impersonal about it, but already he could feel the resolve weakening within him.

"Maybe I don't," he said softly.

He saw her tense. She seemed to draw back and her head cocked a little to one side as if she were regarding him from a new and different perspective.

"Don't joke with me about it, Harland." She sounded hurt. Her head bent now. "It means too much to me to joke about it."

He said nothing. She was a while like that, her head bowed, her hands pressing tightly against her thighs, as if she were immersed in thought. When she spoke, she did not raise her face.

"I don't feel too good about it myself, Harland. Can't you imagine how I must feel? Here I am, hope-lessly in love with you, and there is all that talk about you having killed my husband, and when I ask you about it you always say you don't know. There are times when I'm convinced you did kill him and then I tell myself I should hate you, but I just can't, Har-land, I love you. Even though it's wrong, I love you. Even if you were to tell me Jim was dead by your own hand, I would still love you." Her head lifted now. Her eyes seemed alive with a strange, burning luminosity. "What can I say to make you believe me, Harland? What can I say to convince you that I really love you? What can I do to make you tell me what I want to know?"

Harland did not say anything right off. He just sat

there, staring at her and listening to the hammering of his heart. He did not know if the time was right for it but, finally, he said:

"What do you know about your husband's part in the Border Pacific hold-up?"

He saw her stiffen. The appeal went out of her face. She appeared wary and alert. "Why do you ask that?"

"I've got a reason," he said. He stared at her a moment in silence. Then he continued, "Did you know beforehand that he was going to pull the stick-up?"

She lowered her glance and turned her palms upward and seemed to study them. "I didn't know exactly what Jim had in mind. He had started hanging around with Ike Gibson and Bronco Curtis, and I knew they were no good and so I suspected they were up to something. But I had no idea it was going to be a train hold-up until after it was done."

"Have you any idea why your husband did a thing like that?"

She stared at him queryingly. "What are you driving at, Harland?"

"Did he need money bad? Did he have any debts?"

She seemed to hesitate, then she said, "The First National Bank in Edenville still has a mortgage on this place, I don't think we could ever have paid it off." She hesitated again. Then she took a deep breath and plunged on, "All right, Harland, I'll get it off my chest. Jim and I were through around here. The ranch was losing money. In time we would lose the ranch, too. Jim brooded about it. He wanted to go somewhere away from here and start all over again. But he needed a stake. So he held up that B.P. train."

"Were you in favour of going away from here?" asked Harland.

A pensive look came into her face. Her eyes stared beyond him, into a great, unfathomable distance. "I suppose I did dream of a fresh start somewhere else. I dreamed of a big ranch with big herds and a big house like Bridlebit's. Every woman has dreams like that, Harland, but most of the time that's all they are—just dreams."

Harland said quietly, "Have you any idea why your husband double-crossed Gibson and Curtis?"

Her glance pulled back to him sharply. Her lips tightened ever so slightly. "That I wouldn't know, Harland."

"Where is the money from the hold-up?"

Her eyes narrowed until they were pinpoints of wariness and calculation. Her nostrils pinched. "What makes you think I know where the money is?"

"He was your husband. Didn't he tell you?"

She settled back and stared at him thoughtfully for a while. Then she said slowly, "Let me put it like this, Harland. If I knew where the money was, do you think Gibson and Curtis would have let me alone?" She leaned towards him now, her voice taut with emotion. "I often wish I knew where that money was. Do you think I'd hang around here then? What have I got here, Harland? A poverty ranch and broken dreams and ugly memories. If I had that money—a hundred thousand dollars, Harland—I wouldn't be wasting my life away here in the Stalwarts."

Harland could hear the swift, excited beating of his heart. There was a cloying ache in his throat that made his voice a little harsh. "If I knew where that money was, Lorraine, would you go away with me?"

She drew in her breath in a sharp, audible inhalation. Her shoulders squared back, she was as taut as an iron rod. Her eyes probed at him with an almost physical impact.

"Do you really know where it is, Harland?" she asked hoarsely.

Harland nodded. He kept his glance locked with hers.

"How did you find out, Harland?"

"I'd rather not tell you."

"Why not?"

Harland paused. He wanted to select his words with care. "Isn't it time we started to forget about it, Lorraine? It's no good for you and it's no good for me, this business of always talking about your husband. You say it doesn't make any difference to you whether I killed Lancaster. Do you mean that?"

She dipped her head once. She said nothing. He could see the deep and even rise and fall of her breasts as she breathed. Speculation was strong in the glint in her eyes.

"Then why should it matter," he went on, "how I found out where the money is? The only thing I want to know is this—will you go away with me?"

"How do I know you have the money?" she asked.

"I don't have it. I just said I know where it is."

"Where is it?"

He smiled faintly. "Wouldn't it be better if I just showed you where it is?"

"Will you really show me?"

His smile turned a little sour. "Don't you believe anything I tell you, Lorraine?" Before she could reply, he continued, "There's one easy way for you to find out. Just come with me. We can go in the morning."

She knelt there with her hands resting lightly on

her thighs. Her eyes moved past him once more and that look of wary thoughtfulness came into them. She made no answer to him. She seemed to be reviewing with extreme care all that he had said. Whether she believed any or all of it, she did not say.

After a while, Harland said, "Everyone in the Stalwarts seems to want to know why I came here. You yourself asked me that several times, Lorraine. Isn't all that money a logical reason?"

She withdrew her attention from her thoughts and put it on Harland. "Did you say in the morning, Harland?"

He nodded.

She took a deep breath. She edged a little closer to him and her eyes grew bold. "Am I too mercenary for you, Harland?" she asked huskily. "Do I put too much emphasis on that money? Do I scare you, Harland?"

He felt his throat go dry. "I don't mind."

She leaned still closer to him. "It's just that I want to get away from here so much, Harland. I couldn't bear to have you trick me. It isn't a trick, is it, Harland?"

"Why would it be a trick?"

Then he could think only of her nearness, of the desire he had always experienced for her. It was all there overwhelmingly in him. The guilt and the feeling of evil he pushed far back in his mind. He tried not to think of them as he embraced her.

Chapter Sixteen

The next morning, at sunrise, Harland went down to the corral and saddled both the bay and the pinto. Then he led the horses from the enclosure and waited. He put his back to the corral bars and built a smoke and drew on it thoughtfully.

The day was beginning in that almost monotonous pattern of clear and dry. Around the sun the sky was a brazen yellow. Overhead and to the west the sky was blue. There was not a cloud in sight. The pines looked green and cool, but the clumps of grama grass were sickly and meagre.

Harland leaned against the corral, his eyes on the house. He had to wait a little while before Lorraine Lancaster appeared. She approached with a swinging walk that jounced her breasts and jingled the spurs she now wore on the heels of her boots. The wide-brimmed, flat-crowned hat cast a shadow over her face. At first, Harland could make out only the thin line of her mouth. The Bisley swung at her hip and she had a fringed buckskin jacket draped over an arm.

She caught Harland's querying look and smiled, a little archly. "Did you think I wasn't going to come?" she asked dryly.

"You sure took your time," said Harland.

A corner of her mouth twitched. "I—I had some thinking to do," she murmured. She stepped past him and swung up on the pinto.

Harland ground out the butt of his smoke. Then he stepped over to the bay and mounted. He was conscious of Lorraine's eyes on him all the while. He glanced at her.

"Well, let's go," he said. He was feeling rather tired inside.

She had the ends of the lines twisted tightly about her fingers. For a moment, her eyes were gelid and even hostile. "I'm telling you before we begin, Harland. This better be on the level."

"It's on the level," he said.

She held her breath a while, her eyes weighing him, then she let it come gusting out of her. "Which way do we go?" she said.

He did not lead the way but rode beside her. The bay and the pinto moved through the cool, shaded avenues of the pines and after an hour the trees thinned out and the sun came down all the way to the ground. Here it was no warmer than in the pines and Lorraine, who had put on her jacket, did not take it off.

Harland set his sights on the notch that split the mountain ridge ahead and which led to the barren country beyond. When it became apparent to Lorraine that this was where they were heading, she began regarding Harland with a new, sharp interest.

"Won't you tell me yet where we're going?" she asked.

Harland smiled faintly. "You'll know when we get there."

"Won't you even tell me how long it will be before we get there?"

"It'll take most of the day."

She opened her mouth to speak, then changed her mind. She shrugged and rode on in silence. Harland made no attempt to break it. He just did not feel like talking.

They reached the notch in the middle of the day and in another hour they had passed through the break in the mountain to the barren, arid country. The land stretched empty and desolate and full of an inarticulate loneliness. The slopes rolled ever downward and in the great distance shimmered the heat waves that hid the floor of the desert from sight.

A faint apprehension had come over Harland. He turned often in the saddle to cast long, narrowed glances along his backtrail. But he could see nothing to substantiate the sensation that they were being followed. Yet he knew that someone was out there concealed in the wastes, someone with death for Harland in mind. Though Harland saw nothing out of the ordinary, he was positive of this. It left him cold and with a crawling, flinching sensation in his back.

Lorraine noticed his uneasiness. She began to regard him with amusement. "Worried about something, Harland?" she said once.

He just put a grim stare on her and said nothing.

"What are you looking for, Harland?" she persisted.

"Maybe I'm looking for landmarks," he said dryly.

"Oh!" The mirth faded from her eyes. She became quite grave. "Is something wrong, Harland?"

He shrugged. "Not that I can see. But I've been bushwhacked before. I can't get over the feeling."

"Who would want to bushwhack you?"

"Gibson has tried it. Maybe he'll try it again."

A frown came to her face. She seemed to grow thoughtful as she stared at him. After a while, she rose up in her stirrups and cast a look all around her.

"I can't see anything," she said.

"It's when you can't see it that it's bad."

They lapsed into silence once more. The horses moved at a walk, stirring up only a small trace of dust that quickly blew away. The arid desolation seemed to close in tighter about them. The only sounds were the plopping of the horses' hooves in the sand and the mournful squeaking of saddle leather. Not a living thing appeared as Harland kept scanning the land about them, but he could not get over the feeling that they were not alone.

Harland watched until his eyes began to ache. Still nothing showed. The sun glanced with gleaming brightness off the lonely stances of sage and mesquite and the brown and amber outcropping of stones and the warm and glittering sand. This seemed like an eerie, forgotten world, utterly unconcerned at its invasion by living things, yet the distances seemed to hold a hint of malignant mockery as Harland's eyes probed them and saw nothing.

Finally, Lorraine reined in her pinto. She had been leading the way with Harland giving most of his attention to their backtrail. The bay stopped automatically when the pinto did and Lorraine hipped around in her saddle with a look of annoyance on her face.

"Are you sure you know where you're going, Harland?" She sounded cool and a little angry.

The pulse was pounding at Harland's temple. He did not know if it was from the heat and the sun or from a secret awareness of danger. He paid only scant attention to Lorraine. His eyes were concerned mainly with the unfathomable distances.

"I told you it would take most of the day." He said it almost absently.

His eyes searched the land vigilantly. Something was screaming an alarm in his brain, but his eyes could pick up nothing amiss. To Harland's right the ground sloped upward, to his left it slanted downward. The ubiquitous sage seemed to conceal nothing. The clumps of mesquite huddled lonesomely, their bushy branches lifting vaguely at the sky. A good distance up the slope was a group of brown, serrated rocks, arranged by the hand of creation in the shape of a parapet. Harland studied these rocks carefully, but they only jutted there inanimately. They seemed to mock his apprehension.

Finally, he turned his head towards Lorraine and opened his mouth to say something when that intuition of peril shrieked again in his brain. There was a pressing urgency to it this time and even as Harland's glance swept back to the rocks he was yanking the Winchester out from its boot beneath his leg. He spied a sharp glint of glancing sun and waited for no more. Even before the slug whistled above him he was going down on the far side of the bay.

He hit the ground with a thud and began to roll frantically. He could hear the bullets whining over him, he could hear their sodden thunking into the sand. As Harland had quit the saddle, the bay, panicked, had broken away with a great burst of speed. This sudden start by the horse had kicked up a cloud of dust and this served to shield Harland somewhat until he had gained the dubious shelter of a mesquite bush.

He lay there quietly, waiting to catch his breath. The sweat was streaking down his face. He could hear the loud hammering of his heart and there was grit and dust in his mouth. He spat this out and then he lay there and waited. Whoever it was up in that parapet of rocks had stopped shooting. However, the echoes were still rolling faintly down the mountainside.

When his breathing had steadied and the trembling had gone out of his arms and thighs, Harland brushed his hat from his head and chanced a look through the branches of the mesquite which he parted carefully with his hands.

He looked first at the group of stones. Nothing showed up there. The rocks jutted brown and forlorn and apparently empty, but the bushwhacker still lay up there, Harland knew. He stared a long time. Once he caught a flash as of the sun gleaming off a gun barrel but that was all. Whoever it was up there was mighty careful and mighty patient.

Next Harland looked for Lorraine. She was nowhere to be seen, but then he had to be careful and could not raise his head too high for a good look around. He remembered hearing another horse beside his bay taking off in abrupt, frightened flight. That would have been Lorraine on her pinto. It was not unexpected, but Harland thought about it for a while.

Finally, he turned his thoughts to his own predicament. He was not too badly off if all he wanted to do was get out of here. There was enough sage and mesquite to cover him if he cared to withdraw down the slope until he was out of rifle range. He had spotted his bay in the distance. The animal had stopped and was grazing.

Harland parted the mesquite again and studied those rocks up on the slope above him and a plan began to form in his mind. He could see no sign of the bushwhacker's horse. The slope rose for quite some distance above the stones before dropping down on its opposite side. There was nothing on this side of the ridge behind which the bushwhacker could have hidden his mount. He must have left it on the other side of the slope and walked down to the rocks.

Suddenly there was a glint of sun up on the rocks and Harland dropped flat on the ground as three fast slugs tore through the bush. He had finally been spotted, and as the bushwhacker began to probe the mesquite with bullets, Harland grabbed his rifle and his hat and rolled out of there.

He rolled and crawled and scrambled. Whoever it was in the rocks did not give up easily. He also must have had a good supply of shells. He kept plugging away at every slight movement and at every slight glimpse of Harland. But the slugs kept getting wilder and finally they began to fall short and Harland rose to his feet and brandished his Winchester derisively at the rocks.

Then Harland started walking. He made a big circle just out of rifle range of those rocks. Whenever he stepped in too close the bushwhacker would try a shot or two, but the range was too great for accuracy and Harland always jumped back.

At first, the bushwhacker must have surmised that Harland was heading for his bay, but when Harland began circling up the slope some hint of his intent must have dawned on the ambusher. His attempts with his rifle became frantic, he started to waste shells heedlessly as if he were panicked.

Harland grinned without mirth. A vile elation rose in him at the thought that he finally had his man. The slope above the rocks was barren even of sage and mesquite. The bushwhacker must have realised it was too late to fire.

When Harland was opposite the rocks, he dropped on his knees and began to crawl in. He could see the bushwhacker now. He could see the length of him stretched out on the ground. The rocks were no good to him from this direction. He faced Harland and began pumping lead with a wild urgency.

Harland had been making for a small depression, and he threw himself into this as the ambusher opened up with a furious fusillade. He fired until his rifle was empty. While he reloaded, Harland scrambled out of the tiny hole and raced ahead as fast as he could.

He had his rifle ready, the hammer cocked. He could see the other frantically stuffing shells into his rifle. When the bushwhacker threw his rifle to his shoulder, Harland dropped flat and aimed his own Winchester.

He took the great, breath-freezing chance that the bushwhacker was too rattled and frenzied to take careful aim. Harland shoved his cheek against the stock of his Winchester and looked with one eye down the long barrel and tried not to flinch as the bushwhacker opened up. The ambusher got off two swift shots before Harland was satisfied with his aim.

He took the one shot. The sights were dead centre with the bushwhacker's skull. Even as the Winchester roared, the ambusher seemed to shudder. His head ducked abruptly as if he were suddenly tired and then he pitched forward. He convulsed once in his death

throes, his body heaving up in the air, his arms fling-
ing wide as if to embrace and hold the life fleeing
from him. The convulsion spun him around and he
came down on his back. His arms never did close.
They remained flung out wide on the sand.

Harland's heart was beating in a dull, leaden way
as he rose to his feet. The muscles of his thighs were
trembling and there was a sick feeling in his entrails
as he started forward. He kept the Winchester cocked
and at his hip, but there was no need for this. Expe-
rience told Harland that the bushwhacker was dead.

The man lay sprawled out with his head pointing
down the slope. His eyes were open with only the
whites showing. The mouth was slacked open horribly in a crooked, yawning grimace of agony. The bullet had smashed into his forehead and emerged from
the back of his skull. Beneath his head a tiny carmine
pool was forming on the sand. That was the only
mark of violence on him. His fine clothes were soiled
with sand and dust and the sharp crease was obliter-
ated from his trousers at the knees due to all the time
he had knelt behind his parapet of stones. But, of
course, the condition of his clothing mattered nothing
to him now.

The dead man was Ace Lowrie.

Harland walked down to his bay. Then he mounted
and with a growing reluctance scouted around until
he picked up the tracks of Lorraine Lancaster's pinto.
He sent the bay in pursuit of the tracks, but he did
not push the horse very hard.

Lowrie's death added up to all those other facts
which Harland had assimilated in his mind. It clicked
neatly in place, a precise fit in the ugly, vile pattern
that was now clear in his mind.

The bay moved on. The tracks led in the direction of that abandoned ranch where Harland had suffered so much torture at Worthington's hands. The memory of this was a searing ache in Harland's heart, but he plodded on. He thought of Lancaster and Mitch Antrim and of how they had died and why they had died, and this made it a little easier for him.

The sun was at its three-quarter mark. Harland could feel its mordant heat boring at his back. Even the mesquite and sage, which now grew sparser and lonelier, seemed to shrivel and shrink beneath the beat of the sun. This was all the land seemed to contain, the imperial, merciless sun, this and a lamenting loneliness.

First of all it was but a speck in the distance. A trick of the sun and the dazzling heat, Harland thought, and he moved the bay on, narrowly eyeing the far-off apparition. It appeared to shimmy and weave endlessly, and then all at once it coalesced and Harland saw it was real.

He let the bay move on. A choking sensation came into Harland's throat. His heart quickened, a rush of distaste almost overwhelmed him, but he had guessed all along it was not going to be anything pleasant and he let the bay move on.

Now he could make them out—two people on a rise of ground, two people facing towards him, two people waiting for him. Sand yielded with soft, sucking noises beneath the bay's hooves. Saddle leather squeaked and the sound was sad and mourning in all that stillness.

Ahead, the two waited.

Harland passed the back of a hand over his eyes, wiping the sweat from them. Almost unconsciously, he loosened the .44 in its holster. Another wave of sickness hit his insides, but it quickly passed and in its place there came the first beginnings of a consuming anger.

The two people ahead did not move. They kept on waiting.

The bay plodded on. It was tired, for it had come a long way with little rest that day, but Harland had little mind for the animal's discomfort. His eyes held only the image of the two ahead.

The bay was close enough now for Harland to recognise the two. Reining in the bay, he sat a while in the kak, watching them. The two were Lorraine Lancaster and Ike Gibson.

Gibson stood behind Lorraine. With his left hand the burly rancher held Lorraine's wrists imprisoned behind her back. Gibson's right hand held his .45. The muzzle of the six-shooter was shoved hard against the small of Lorraine's back.

Gibson waited until the horse and Harland were fifty feet away. Then his harsh voice rang out. "Stop where you are, Harland, or I'll split her spine with my .45!"

Harland reined in the bay. He stepped slowly to the ground. He looped the ends of the lines around the saddlehorn and then he slapped the bay hard on the rump. The animal went off at a run.

Harland stood there and stared narrowly at the two.

Lorraine's face was grey and strained with fright. Her breasts heaved convulsively and her widened eyes stared frantically, beseechingly at him.

Behind her, Ike Gibson's face was parted in a white, grimacing grin. He laughed in brutal triumph, the sound of it bubbling harshly out into the stillness, drowning out Lorraine's laboured, sibilant breathing.

"I've got you right where I want you, Harland,"

Gibson cried. "You got away from me twice. You're not getting away from me now!"

Harland said nothing. The echoes of Gibson's voice went dying down the mountainside, and then Harland could hear his own soft, spaced breathing. He looked at Lorraine's face, at the fear and appeal in it, and a momentary sadness touched him, but the emotion was quickly gone.

"Unbuckle your gunbelt, Harland, and drop it to the ground," shouted Gibson. He laughed coarsely. "I know how you feel about this lady. Drop your belt, Harland, if you don't want her killed!"

Harland kept his hands at his sides. He did not move, he just went on staring at Gibson and Lorraine.

A sudden burst of rage contorted Gibson's face. "Don't you think I mean it?" he bellowed wrathfully. "Do you think I'm afraid to kill her just because she's a woman? I mean to have that money, Harland, and you know where it is. I'm giving you the choice. Tell me where that money is or she dies!"

Lorraine started to struggle, but Gibson gave a hard, brutal shove to his .45 and Lorraine emitted a short, sharp scream of pain and then she was standing still again. Her mouth worked as if she were trying to say something to Harland, but no sounds emerged from her throat.

Harland stood there with his hands slack at his side. He could feel the sweat forming in his palms, he could feel it beading his upper lips. He neither moved nor spoke.

"Damn you, Harland, you hear me?" Gibson shouted angrily and impatiently. "I ain't waiting all day. You drop that belt and then you come up here and tell me where that money is. If I have to kill her, it won't be in a nice way, Harland!"

185

Now Harland moved. His heart seemed to want to jump all the way up into his throat, he could feel his blood chill in his veins, but he started ahead, up the gentle slope, towards Gibson and Lorraine. He had taken three short steps when Gibson bellowed:

"Stand where you are, Harland!" He pressed cruelly with his six-shooter and Lorraine shrieked with agony. Gibson was in a crouch, his eyes glaring past Lorraine down at Harland. "Maybe you didn't hear me right. I said drop your belt first, then come up here. I'm through horsing around, Harland!"

Harland had halted. A spasm passed through his entrails, then all at once he was cold and relentless inside. He took a deep breath and started on again.

Gibson's face darkened, his lips peeled back from his teeth. "I'm warning you for the last time, Harland," he cried. "Don't think I won't kill her. You aren't tricking me this time, Harland. I don't have to worry about winging you. Didn't you hear me? I'll kill her if you take another step!"

Harland moved on. The high heels of his boots dug into the sand, his spurs jingled faintly, mournfully, he took his time going up the gentle slope, he was careful never to be off balance. Just one step at a time, he told himself, one step at a time. He no longer watched Lorraine. His attention was devoted entirely and relentlessly to Ike Gibson.

Gibson's mouth worked, but for the instant only unintelligible sounds emitted. Unbelief registered on his wide face. He licked his lips in nervousness and puzzlement. He could not understand this.

"Goddamn you, Harland," he shouted when he found his voice again. "I'll make sure she dies slow. I won't shoot her clean. I'll bust her spine for her and then she can hang on a long time before she goes. Did you hear me, Harland?''

One step at a time, Harland told himself, one step at a time. He refused to think of anything else. His eyes never left Gibson's face. He could see the bewilderment and confusion there. Just one step at a time. . . .

"By damn," Gibson cried, "you do think I'm bluffing, don't you?" He shook his huge head as if this did not make sense to him. "I won't open my mouth again, Harland. For the last time, stop and drop your belt!''

Harland moved on. His heart was beating with short, quick strokes. There was sweat on his face, there was sweat under his armpits, there was sweat trickling down his back, but he was all cold inside. One step at a time. Just one step at a time. . . .

Gibson's chest swelled as he took a prodigious breath. "All right," he growled, as the breath came gusting out. "You asked for it."

Lorraine sensed it coming and she gave a sudden, strong jerk that for a moment pulled her back away from the muzzle of Gibson's gun. But she did not pull away far enough. The .45 blasted and Lorraine screamed hoarsely. The instant he fired Gibson released his hold on her wrists. She went tumbling on her face on the ground.

Harland saw it coming. There was both regret and relief in him as Gibson's gun blasted. Harland drew. Rage blazed across his brain as he saw Lorraine fall. This was what he had wanted, this was what he had deliberately brought about, but still the wrath surged in him.

As Gibson pushed Lorraine from him and whirled to meet Harland, Harland fired. The slug took Gibson in the chest. The force of it rocked him back a step. It looked like he was going down, but he braced his legs and threw his left arm out and retained his balance. The .45 had dropped in his right hand but now the gun started to lift.

Harland fired a second time. This slug smashed into Gibson's left shoulder. It spun him half around, his face grimacing with agony. His gun roared but the bullet went harmlessly into the ground. Gibson's legs wavered, but he would not go down. He began to bring his .45 up again.

Harland's third shot took Gibson in the left side. With his left hand he clutched the spot where he had been hit and blood began to ooze between his clenched, pressing fingers. He began to sob with pain and frustration.

Harland fired again. The fourth slug slammed into Gibson's belly. This was all the punishment his legs could take. His knees buckled and hit the ground, but Gibson did not go all the way. He knelt there, gasping and retching with pain. The .45 was still in his hand but he did not seem to know what to do with it.

Harland was crying now. He did not know if it was from grief or relief or anger. Maybe it was all mixed together, or maybe it was only sweat stinging his eyes. Fury spasmed in him and screamed in his brain.

His fifth shot smashed Gibson's right shoulder and the .45 fell from his hand. Still Gibson would not go all the way down. He rocked there on his knees, gasping and wheezing with hurt, his right hand pawing weakly and futilely on the ground for the .45 it had lost.

Harland's sixth and last shot entered Gibson's forehead, passed through his brain and emerged from the back of his skull. This time he went down. He toppled over gently, like a tired man laying himself down to sleep. And sleep Gibson would, for a long, long time.

Chapter Seventeen

Now that it was over, Harland stood there, trembling with reaction. The muscles of his thighs kept shuddering and he did not think that his knees could hold him up, but in a little while these sensations passed. He punched the empty cartridges from his .44 and reloaded with fresh shells.

With an effort, he had restrained himself from glancing at Lorraine. Now he could no longer hold back. She lay as she had fallen, stretched flat on the sand, with her head turned to one side, one cheek pressed against the earth. He walked slowly, reluctantly over to her. She did not stir. She did not seem to hear him. The thought struck Harland that she was dead, but then he saw her lips flutter slightly and he knew that she still breathed.

He bent down and rolled her on her back. Her arms flopped loosely and her eyes stayed closed, but she moaned as the movement brought her pain and her lips mumbled unintelligibly. Then something choked in her throat and she began to cough. A trickle of blood came out of the corner of her mouth by the time she stopped coughing.

Harland stood and stared down at her. He wondered that he should feel so distant and indifferent inside. The bullet which had entered Lorraine's back had emerged from her chest. The front of her skirt was covered with blood. Her face was grey and looked very tired. She appeared to be hungering for that long rest which was not far off for her.

Harland made no attempt to examine her wound or to bind it. He kept remembering Lancaster and Antrim.

The whinny of a horse roused Harland from his preoccupation. He turned and saw that his bay had returned to join the pinto and Gibson's buckskin. Slowly, Harland walked over to the horses. He unsaddled the pinto and the buckskin and stripped off their bridles. Then he took the bay's lines and led the horse back to where Lorraine lay.

Her eyes were open now. She saw Harland and on the instant she frowned, then she tried to smile. "Oh, Harland, Harland," she breathed. "You're all right, aren't you, Harland?"

He said nothing. He just went on staring down at her.

She frowned again as if she were remembering something that was quite an effort to recall. "Why did you do it, Harland?" she asked weakly, piteously. "You knew he would shoot me. Why did you do it?"

He took something out of the pocket of his shirt and for an instant he weighed the object in his hand, his eyes steady on hers. "When I killed your husband," he told her slowly so that she would understand every word, "I promised myself that one day I would return every penny I was paid to the one who had hired me." He dropped the thing in his hand so that it fell on her chest. "Here it is, Lorraine."

She did not comprehend immediately. She frowned and a hand picked weakly at the packet of greenbacks on her chest. Then understanding dawned on her. Resentment flared in her fevered eyes and she tried to come up on one elbow, but the attempt was too much for her. She fell back, gasping and choking. When she could speak, she said:

"That's a terrible thing to accuse me of, Harland. Jim was my husband. I loved him. How can you even think that I would hire someone to kill him?"

"The way he died told me that. It took me a little time to figure it out but I finally got there, Lorraine. You see, I gave your husband an even break. That was something you and Elliott hadn't banked on. You figured a hired killer would let your husband have it in the back. Well, I'm not that kind of a hired killer.

"Another thing you didn't bank on was that your husband had been tipped off he had been marked down to die. A woman named Lily Sinclair who worked in the Ace of Diamonds tipped him off somehow. Anyway, he knew what was coming. He knew who had hired me to kill him. He beat me to the draw, Lorraine." He was starting to sweat again. Remembrance of it always did that to him, it seemed. "He was faster than me and he could have dropped me cold, but he had chosen to die. He let me kill him instead. I tried to get him to tell me before he died who it was that had really hired me. He wouldn't say because he still loved you. But I should have known it was you when I got to the Stalwarts and found out that he was married. He lived several hours after I shot him. He was delirious most of the time and he talked a lot about his mother and when he was a kid. But he never mentioned you, Lorraine. The hurt was so big in him he never mentioned your name. That's the thing that should have told me right away who it was behind his death."

"No, no, Harland," she moaned, shaking her head. "You've got it all wrong. I loved him. I married him, didn't I? I had the choice of any man in the Stalwarts but I picked Jim. Doesn't that prove I loved him? He had nothing, yet I married him. Would I have done that if I didn't love him?"

"Love has a way of ending as well as beginning," he said, thinking also of himself.

"All right, Harland, all right," she said, speaking with effort. "If I can't convince you that way, let me put it like this. If I'd had Jim killed, what was there to prevent me from killing you and putting you out of the way? I had lots of chances, you know."

"That's right," he admitted, "but that was your big stumbling block. You see, Lorraine, you couldn't figure out why I had come to the Stalwarts. It didn't make sense to you that I'd kill your husband and then come here to avenge him. Since his body wasn't found, you couldn't be sure that he was dead. There was the chance that he'd found out your scheme and that he'd bought me out in turn and sent me here to the Stalwarts to see if what he suspected was true. That's why you tried so hard to find out from me if he was really dead," he said bitterly. "That's why you pretended to be in love with me."

"I didn't pretend," she whispered, tears in her eyes. "I do love you, Harland."

"Maybe you do," he said. "Maybe you love me

like you loved your husband, but I don't want that kind of love. It ends too fast and too rough. It's too selfish a love.''

''Oh, Harland, Harland, you don't know what you're saying.''

''I know, all right,'' he said. His lips moved stiffly. There was only gall and distaste in his heart. ''You're incapable of really loving anyone, Lorraine. You only love someone for what you can get out of him. It was like that for you with Lancaster and Antrim and, yes, even Lowrie.''

She turned her face to the side, away from him. A spasm of pain convulsed her and ripped a hoarse moan out of her. Then she began to cry, softly. ''I'm hurt and sick and suffering and you stand there accusing me of dirty, filthy things. Don't you have a heart, Harland?''

''I have one,'' he said, ''but I know when to use it. You are all through fooling me, Lorraine. I've seen too much of your work to be fooled any more. Now I don't know too much about your husband but I don't think he was all bad. I know he was good with a gun.'' He sweated a little. ''But that doesn't mean anything. He tried to make a go of it in a decent, honest way, but that wasn't enough for you. You wanted money fast and you wanted it in big piles. He knew he was losing you and so he threw in with Gibson and Curtis and held up that Border Pacific train. But you weren't satisfied with a third of a hundred thousand dollars. You got him to double-cross his pals and keep the money all for himself. Naturally, he couldn't stay around here any more with Gibson and Curtis wanting their share, so he turned the money over to you and left. You were supposed to follow with the money when he was safe somewhere.

But you had planned something better. You and Lowrie.''

She kept her face averted. "Lies, lies,'' she moaned. "All lies.''

"I know you and how you work, Lorraine,'' he said, "and so I can figure out how it was. Lowrie was the one for you, wasn't he? Oh, the two of you were clever about it, you were careful never to be seen together, but it was Lowrie in with you all the time, wasn't it? He was at your place yesterday before I got there, wasn't he? You left a note for him to follow us and kill me, didn't you? Don't bother denying it, Lorraine, because I won't believe you.''

She turned her face and stared wide-eyed at him now. Her breasts heaved with the labour of her breathing.

"Three men died to protect you, Lorraine,'' he went on, counting them off on his fingers. "Jim Lancaster, Ace Lowrie and Mitch Antrim!''

"Mitch?''

"Yeh, Mitch,'' he said angrily, bitterly. "I killed him yesterday morning. He knew I was getting close to figuring it out. He had always loved you but you have never given him a tumble. Still, that didn't mean anything to Mitch. He knew what you'd done to your husband, he knew what you were, but he still loved you. So he faced me and told me he had had me hired to kill Lancaster so he could have you. Then he drew on me and I had to kill him. I didn't have the heart to tell him I didn't believe a word he had told me. So he died happy, Lorraine.''

"No, Harland, no,'' she said, starting to shake her head again. "It wasn't at all like that. You've got it all wrong.''

"I've got it right,'' he said. "Mitch was the one

who made me see how it was. He died to protect you because he loved you that much. If he loved you that way, couldn't your husband have loved you just as much? If it had been anyone else behind Lancaster's death, he'd have killed me and then come back here to square things. But he loved you too much. He knew he had lost you for good, so he didn't care to live any more. Even Lowrie in his selfish way tried to take the blame to protect you. Even he died for you, Lorraine. All these died for you so that you could have a hundred thousand dollars.''

"I don't know anything about that money, Harland,'' she insisted weakly. "If I did, would I have gone with you this morning? If I had that money, would I have listened to you and then gone away with you?''

"You had to play it this way, Lorraine,'' he told her. "You had to pretend you didn't know where the money was and that you were looking for it, because if Gibson had suspected you knew where that money was—Well, you know what he did just to try to get me to talk. You played it smart, Lorraine,'' he said with sarcastic praise. "Too smart.''

He picked up the bay's lines. Lorraine saw this and she said, "What are you doing, Harland?''

"I'm riding.''

"You aren't going to leave me?''

"That's right.''

"No, Harland, no. Please stay with me.''

He looked down at her. Five minutes, that was all she had left. But he didn't want to give her even that.

"Just one thing, Harland. That's all I want.''

"What is it?''

Her mouth moved, her lips formed a small "o,''

but the eyes still were pain-filled, fever-filled. Something else, too.

"All I want, Harland. Please kiss me before you go." She made the small "o" again, and her tongue slowly moved over her lips. It was laboured and frightful.

He shrugged his shoulders and moved away from the horse. He stood over her for a long minute and then he bent down and kissed her, his eyes closed. He didn't want to see it. And then he froze.

Maybe he should have guessed. It was all there to know, but somehow all the years had played tricks and now when he needed them, when he needed the speed and skill and killer-instinct, they weren't there.

He felt her do it, even as his lips brushed against the rounded mouth. The hand that crawled to his side, and clumsily, heavily, slowly pulled his gun from its holster and pressed it against his side, firm and sure as death. And he opened his eyes and saw hers, inches away, blazing with hate. That was the something else he had seen there, but he hadn't guessed.

Still, he knew, it didn't have to be. Though the gun was firm, planted in his side, he knew he could slash down, hit the wrist, divert the shot she would get off, save himself.

Save himself. That was the bit that held him. Save himself for what? For the years ahead, for the gun money they would keep shoving at him. "Work, killer. Do your job. Here's your wages." The empty, dark maw of years ahead, bleak and beckoning, unchanging. Save himself, for that.

But now he could change it all.

Now he had his chance, to do the only decent thing he could to a life that had twisted away and gone wrong.

Now he knew, at last, why Lancaster had waited when he had him beaten. What was the use?

He relaxed and pressed his mouth against hers once more, and closed his eyes, and very soon the blackness came over them both. . . .

DON'T MISS OTHER CLASSIC LEISURE WESTERNS!

High Prairie by Hiram King. Cole Granger doesn't have much in this world. A small spread is just about all he can call his own. That and his honor. So when he gives his word that he'll deliver some prize horses to a neighbor, he'll be damned before he'll let those horses escape. And anything that gets between Cole and the horses will regret it.

___4324-6 $3.99 US/$4.99 CAN

Stillwater Smith by Frank Roderus. There are two kinds of men on the frontier. There's the kind who is tough with a gun in his hand, who preys on anyone weaker than himself. Then there is Stillwater Smith, who doesn't take easily to killing, but who is always ready to fight for what he believes in. And there's only so far you can push him.

___4306-8 $3.99 US/$4.99 CAN

THE LAST WARPATH

**"The most critically acclaimed Western writer of this or
any other time!"**
—Loren D. Estleman

The battle between the U.S. Cavalry and the wild-riding
Cheyenne, lords of the North Prairie, rages across the
Western plains for forty years. The white man demands
peace or total war, and the Cheyenne will not pay the price
of peace. Great leaders like Little Wolf and Dull Knife know
their people are meant to range with the eagle and the wolf.
The mighty Cheyenne will fight to be free until the last
warrior has gone forever upon the last warpath.

**FIVE-TIME WINNER OF THE
GOLDEN SPUR AWARD**

MACKENNA'S GOLD

WILL HENRY

"Some of the best writing the American West can claim!"

—Brian Garfield, Bestselling Author of
Death Wish

Somewhere in 100,000 square miles of wilderness is the fabled Lost Canyon of Gold. With his dying breath, an ancient Apache warrior entrusts Glen Mackenna with the location of the lode that will make any man—or woman— rich beyond their wildest dreams. Halfbreed renegade and captive girl, mercenary soldier and thieving scout—brave or beaten, innocent or evil, they'll sell their very souls to possess Mackenna's gold.

_4154-5 $4.50 US/$5.50 CAN

Gold In California!

TODHUNTER BALLARD

Winner Of The Golden Spur Award

Gold Fever! Some call it madness, some a fantasy. Yet the promise of untold wealth draws people west like bees to honey.

Determined to strike the mother lode, young Austin Garner and his family set out to cross the untamed American continent. The going is brutal—nearly three thousand miles of desert, disease, and death—and without extraordinary strength and courage, the pioneers will surely perish.

But California is the greatest challenge of all: a sprawling, unforgiving land full of scoundrels and scalawags, claim jumpers and con men, failures and fortunes. Yet Garner and his kin are ready to sacrifice life and love to realize their dream of gold in California!

_3888-9 $4.99 US/$6.99 CAN

WILL HENRY

JOURNEY TO SHILOH

While the bloody War Between the States is ripping the country apart, Buck Burnet can only pray that the fighting will last until he can earn himself a share of the glory. Together with a ragtag band of youths who call themselves the Concho County Comanches, Buck sets out to drive the damn Yankees out of his beloved Confederacy. But the trail from the plains of Texas to the killing fields of Tennessee is full of danger. Buck and his comrades must fight the uncontrollable fury of nature and the unfathomable treachery of men. And when the brave Rebels finally meet up with their army, they must face the greatest challenge of all: a merciless battle against the forces of Grant and Sherman that will truly prove that war is hell.

___4203-7 $4.50 US/$5.50 CAN

Available by mail from

PEOPLE OF THE LIGHTNING • Kathleen O'Neal Gear and W. Michael Gear

The next novel in the First North American series by best-selling authors Kathleen O'Neal Gear and W. Michael Gear.

RELIC • Douglas Preston and Lincoln Child

Alien meets *Jurassic Park* in New York City!

MAGNIFICENT SAVAGES • Fred Mustard Stewart

From China's opium trade to Garibaldi's Italy to the New York of Astor and Vanderbilt, comes this blockbuster, 19th century historical novel of the clipper ships and the men who made them.

WORLD WITHOUT END • Molly Cochran and Warren Murphy

"In this exciting adventure the mysterious island is artfully combined with the Bermuda Triangle and modern day life."—VOYA

A MAN'S GAME • Newton Thornburg

Another startling thriller from the author of *Cutter and Bone*, which *The New York Times* called "the best novel of its kind in ten years!"

SPOOKER • Dean Ing

It took the government a long time to figure out that someone was killing agents for their spookers—until that someone made one fatal mistake.

WHITE SMOKE • Andrew M. Greeley

Only Andrew M. Greeley, Catholic priest and bestselling novelist, could have written this blockbuster tale about what *might* happen when the next Pope must be chosen and the fate of the Church itself hangs in the balance.